A working vacation

The wind picked up off the bay, and Harriet shivered. "We spotted you girls in line, and you looked awfully cold," she said, speaking for herself. "The cafés at Ghirardelli have divine hot chocolate."

I said, "That sounds nice, except we're about to catch the next boat tour of the harbor."

"Oh, come on!" Ed pleaded. "It's only eleven in the morning. There's plenty of time left in the day. That boat ride only takes an hour."

Bess shrugged. "I wouldn't mind sampling some San Francisco hot chocolate. And the weather might get warmer by the time we finish."

"Very true, dear," Harriet said. "No need to put up with unnecessary discomfort while sightseeing. Just listening to a tour guide can be torture enough."

As we followed Ed and Harriet toward Ghirardelli Square, George bent her head toward me and whispered, "Can you believe Harriet called Bess dear? I mean, up till now she's been a tough nut to crack."

"Something's up with her," I muttered back.

And no sooner were we sipping our hot chocolate in a toasty café that smelled of coffee and croissants, than Harriet pulled out the biggest surprise of the day. . . .

NANCY DREW
girl detective™

Available from Aladdin Paperbacks

NANCY DREW

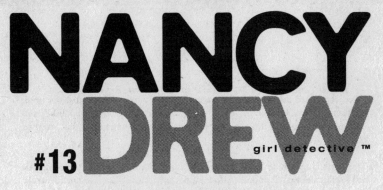

DREW

girl detective ™

#13

Trade Wind Danger

CAROLYN KEENE

Aladdin Paperbacks

New York   London   Toronto   Sydney

This book is a work of fiction. Any references to historical events, real people, or real locales are used fictitiously. Other names, characters, places, and incidents are the product of the author's imagination, and any resemblance to actual events or locales or persons, living or dead, is entirely coincidental.

❧ ALADDIN PAPERBACKS
An imprint of Simon & Schuster Children's Publishing Division
1230 Avenue of the Americas, New York, NY 10020
Copyright © 2005 by Simon & Schuster, Inc.
All rights reserved, including the right of
reproduction in whole or in part in any form.
NANCY DREW is a registered trademark of Simon & Schuster, Inc.
ALADDIN PAPERBACKS, NANCY DREW: GIRL DETECTIVE, and
colophon are trademarks of Simon & Schuster, Inc.
Designed by Lisa Vega
The text of this book was set in Bembo.
Manufactured in the United States of America
First Aladdin Paperbacks edition September 2005
10
Library of Congress Control Number 2004116369
ISBN 0-689-87641-6

Contents

Trade Wind Danger

Mysterious Strangers

San Francisco is the most beautiful city I've ever seen—and that's saying a lot, because I've also seen Paris. Anyway, here I was on a cool spring morning, having just arrived with my two best friends, George Fayne and Bess Marvin. And I couldn't imagine anything better.

"Are you sure you have enough suitcases, Bess?" George asked, eyeing Bess's four designer suitcases piled on the porter's trolley outside our hotel. "I'm worried you've forgotten something."

"Me? Forget *clothes*?" Bess replied, ignoring her cousin's sarcasm. "Impossible." She dug a light jacket from one of her bags and pulled it over her tank top. Shaking back her blond hair, she added, "My guide-book warned that San Francisco weather can be crazy—sunny, rainy, cold, and warm, all in the same day. I don't want to be caught unprepared."

"My motto is One Vacation, One Backpack," George said, setting her backpack next to my duffel bag on the trolley. "Two pairs of jeans, shorts, T-shirts, and a rainproof sweatshirt. How is that not prepared?"

I smiled as my two friends teased each other. Even though Bess and George are cousins, they couldn't be more different. Bess is blond, sweet, and stylish, without a competitive bone in her body. Dark-haired George has a dry wit, shrugs at the mention of a clothing sale, and as for competitive bones—well, let's just say she's one of the best athletes I've ever known. But Bess and George are alike in this way: They're devoted to each other, and to me.

"Got everything, girls?" the elderly cab driver asked after I paid him. "You'll love San Francisco. You may even leave your hearts here," he added, paraphrasing a line from an old song. "Anyway, you're sure to meet some odd ducks. All sorts of colorful characters flock to this city. It attracts them. Anyway, toodle-oo!" He waved out the window as he drove away.

"The characters in San Francisco seem almost as colorful as the ones in River Heights," George commented as we watched the cab race another one up a nearby hill. "I mean, does that guy realize he's pushing eighty?"

"This place is famous for its eccentrics," I said, "like the beatniks in the nineteen fifties."

"Hippies in the sixties," Bess chimed in.

"And don't forget all the techies who invented new computer systems in their garages later on," George said.

"I bet you'll find a mystery on this vacation, Nancy," Bess said. "If this city is so wild and crazy, there must be tons of them around."

I smiled. I couldn't help myself. The thought of tons of mysteries surrounding me was exciting. Hey, I'm a detective. What can I say?

Suddenly, an object whizzed by me, missing my head by inches. I whirled around, following it with my eyes as it continued its bouncy descent down the street to our right.

"A tennis ball!" George exclaimed.

"Thrown on purpose?" Bess asked nervously.

"Doubt it, miss," the porter said. "Probably some kid playing. Impossible to catch a ball once it gets going down one of these hills. Just be glad it wasn't a skateboard, or a car with failed brakes. 'Course, when an earthquake comes, a car with no brakes seems like a piece of cake."

"I guess we're living dangerously just by standing on the street," Bess said.

"Then let's go in," George suggested. "The sooner

we get settled, the sooner we can start exploring this awesome city."

We followed the porter into the lobby and glanced around. Our hotel, the Old Bay Mare, was adorable. Originally someone's Victorian house, the place was decorated in floral wallpaper and antique furniture. After we checked in, the porter showed us to a cozy room with twin brass beds, a cot, and a cheerful fire that crackled away as if it had been waiting all morning to greet us.

We tipped him and closed the door. Bess flopped down on the cot. "I'll take this bed. I don't need a fancy one," she offered.

I smiled. Bess may have too much luggage in her life, but you can always trust her to be a good sport.

"Anyway, good night." She shut her eyes.

"What do you mean, 'good night'?" George asked incredulously. "Haven't you noticed the bright sun? What about exploring San Francisco?"

Bess hid her face under the pillow. "You guys go," she said in a muffled voice. "I'm feeling kind of jet-lagged. It was a long flight from Chicago, and the fire feels great."

"It's too hot and it's putting you to sleep," George declared. She bent over Bess and tugged on her arm. "You'll thank me for this, Bess."

"George is right," I said. "If the weather here

changes as much as you say it does, Bess, we'd better take advantage of the sun. Let's check out the sights."

Bess sat up groggily. "Must you use my own words against me, Nancy?" She shrugged. "But what can I expect from the daughter of a successful lawyer?"

I laughed. My father, Carson Drew, was a well-known attorney in River Heights. As usual Bess spoke the truth. Dad has trained me well.

Minutes later we were walking downhill to Union Square, where the hotel desk clerk had told us we could catch one of the famous San Francisco cable cars. Our destination: Fisherman's Wharf, where we planned to board a boat that toured the bay and went by Alcatraz, the old island prison.

"San Francisco!" Bess said with a sigh, her cheeks pink from the bracing walk. "Just the name is romantic."

"Speaking of romance," George said, "too bad Ned had college exams and couldn't join us, Nancy."

"I wish Ned could be here too." Ned's absence caused my heart a momentary twinge, but I rallied. "Don't forget, guys, San Francisco isn't just about romance. It's also about mystery. I mean, the crime writer Dashiell Hammett set many of his books here. Remember that old movie *The Maltese Falcon*? Humphrey Bogart chasing clues through the San Francisco fog?"

My friends didn't answer me—too busy looking at the scenery, I guess.

We rounded the corner. A cable car waited by the side of a small green park nearby.

"That cable car looks just like the one in the ad," Bess said, referring to a tourist brochure we'd picked up at our hotel. An old-fashioned brown trolleylike car, it had wooden seats lining the inside and large windows opening behind the seats. There were step platforms and poles outside the car for adventurous passengers who would rather hang on. Unfortunately all those spots were taken.

Before we climbed aboard, Bess peeked under the car. Typical Bess behavior—she absolutely *must* know how machines work. As far as I could tell, the car was attached to a cable buried in the street, and the driver maneuvered a lever that looked like a brake.

The cable car bell rang out merrily.

"I think that means we're supposed to hurry and get on," George said as we scrambled onto the packed car.

"Yeah, but how?" Bess asked. "People are crammed like sardines in here." She held her breath as she tried to fit into a tight space between two teenagers.

I squeezed in next to an older couple, bumping into the small woman. "Oh, sorry," I said.

Instead of replying, she gave me a hard stare. Not the reaction I was expecting.

The conductor interrupted my thoughts by taking our fare. Even he—a pro at this job—was having a hard time working his way through the crowd.

"Maybe we should have waited for the next one," Bess said in a strained voice. "I can't breathe."

"The other cars would have been just as crowded, young lady," said the man next to me. "It's the tourists."

I glanced at the man. Tall and distinguished, he had salt-and-pepper hair and a high-wattage smile. I would have stepped backward from the brightness if space had allowed.

The man went on. "I'm a San Francisco resident myself. My wife, Harriet, and I rarely ride these cars. But we'd just finished our shopping near Union Square when this one arrived, and since we were eager to head home, I thought it made sense to hop on it. Don't you agree, darling?" he added, glancing at the gray-haired woman.

Harriet pursed her lips. For a moment I was in suspense. Would she answer him? Her face was as solemn as the Sphinx's.

Then she shrugged. "Certainly, Ed. You are always so sensible."

Ed laughed. "I try to be."

"Have you lived here all your lives?" I asked Harriet. I can't help my nosy questions. Maybe that's why

I'm a detective. I was just curious to see if I could get her to talk.

Harriet narrowed her silvery eyes. The moment of silence dragged on. Unlike her friendly husband, she obviously preferred to keep her thoughts to herself—at least around strangers.

"We've lived here for five years," Ed said. "Moved from New York. San Francisco is a wonderful place. Just the right size. Haunting scenery. The beauty speaks for itself. Plus there's plenty of culture, and easy access to the outdoors if you like hiking or boating or whatnot. I never feel cooped up in San Francisco."

"Not even now?" George asked. "You must admit this cable car is a bit tight."

"Ah, well," Ed said. "I don't mind it. I'm still free. I can get off at any time."

The cable car started a steep ascent. I could feel my weight—and everyone else's—move toward the back of the car. If I didn't know better, I'd think the car was about to flip over. I'm only slightly exaggerating when I say we were now perpendicular to the ground.

I craned my neck around a group of riders and looked outside. The hill was so steep that it blocked my view of the sky. All I saw was a row of colorful Victorian houses lining the side of the street. Palm trees swayed in a few front yards.

"I can't believe it. That sidewalk has stairs!" Bess exclaimed.

"Some of our hills are too steep for regular sidewalks," Ed explained. "You need steps to climb them. By the way, where are you girls from?"

"River Heights," Bess answered. "It's not far from Chicago. We flew in from there this morning. We're here on vacation. Ever since Nancy read some mysteries by Dashiell Hammett, she's wanted to come here. She persuaded us to come along too."

Ed smiled. "A nice city, Chicago. You've got that lovely lake. Still, I prefer San Francisco. The hills, the fog . . . I could go on."

But he couldn't. The cable car jerked to a stop, and exclamations of surprise erupted around us, drowning out all conversation. "Are we picking up more passengers in the middle of the hill?" someone asked.

I checked to see. As I suspected, we were nowhere near a cable car stop. But I didn't suspect danger until I saw Harriet's stony expression change. She cast an anxious glance at the cable car controls.

The driver wasn't there.

With a slight whispering sound, the cable car began to slide backward. Fifty feet below us, a red SUV struggled to turn out of our way.

2

Bess's Fortune

A kid laughed. "This is just like the Lazy Loop at the fair!"

But I knew this was no amusement park ride. As we picked up speed, the laughing stopped abruptly, only to be replaced by screams of panic. George's brown eyes widened into a terrified stare as she caught my anxious gaze.

"Let me through!" Bess shouted, elbowing her way to the back of the car. The crowd pressed tight, hindering her progress. "Please, get out of my way. There's a brake back there!"

The crowd didn't question her. Full of hope, people parted as much as possible to let Bess through, while the SUV below us struggled to turn into a row of cars waiting at a stop light. "Go, Bess!"

I shouted. To Ed and Harriet, I added, "Our friend knows cars like the back of her hand. If anyone can stop this thing, she can."

Ed and Harriet didn't look reassured. Maybe Bess's feminine appearance made them doubt her—but her machine sense is every bit as sharp as her fashion sense.

I cast a glance below us. My heart sank. The SUV was only twenty feet away. The screams inside the car grew louder. Bess eyed a cranklike control at the back of the car. A split-second was all she needed to reach out and grab it. The cable car jolted to a screeching stop.

Everyone was silent for a few moments, and then burst into cheers.

"Hooray!"

"You saved us!"

"Are you a superhero?" a small boy asked.

"She's an angel!" an old woman declared.

Bess looked embarrassed by all the attention. Her blue eyes glanced down shyly at her feet.

"Good job, miss!" the conductor exclaimed as he plowed through the passengers to join her.

"No thanks to you," a man growled.

"Sorry, everyone," the conductor said, "but I was taking fares in the middle of the car—nothing unusual. What happened to our operator, though?"

The crowd continued to berate the conductor, ignoring the question, as the SUV driver appeared and added his two cents. Ignoring the abuse being hurled at him from all sides, the conductor made sure the rear brake was safely connected. Then he headed to the front of the car. Meanwhile the crowd on the cable car had thinned considerably. Not many passengers wanted to risk a repeat of our backward slide.

I followed the conductor. As we came closer, passengers near the front were clamoring for his attention, speaking all at once and looking freaked.

"Our driver is out cold," a man explained.

"I shook him and he won't respond," confirmed another.

Sure enough, the cable car driver was slumped over the front of the car. I shouted for a doctor, then took out my cell phone to call 911.

"Don't worry—I just called the medics myself, miss," the man who had shaken the driver said, brandishing a cell phone. Cupping his hands beside his mouth, he shouted, "Is anyone here a doctor?"

No one came forward, and that seemed to answer the question, but an ambulance from Bay Hospital arrived within a few seconds. The EMS guys, after giving the driver a quick check, bundled him onto a stretcher. "Looks like he may have had a heart attack," one of the technicians explained as he helped trundle the stretcher off the cable car. "But at least he's still alive. I hope we can save him."

The conductor, who had been talking furiously into a cell phone, took control of the situation by asking all remaining passengers to step off the cable car. "It's out of service for now," he announced. "I advise everyone to take a car on a nearby line. I'm waiting for a substitute driver and a mechanic to arrive, so we can check this one for damage."

The few passengers who were left piled off. "Girls," Ed said, appearing suddenly at my side, "why don't you follow Harriet and me? We'll show you where to catch another car." Several minutes later we arrived at another cable car stop on a different line. While we waited in line with him and Harriet, Ed said, "I sure hope our driver will be okay." Turning to Bess, he added, "Thanks to you, young lady, we're alive to find out. By the way, girls, what are your names?"

"I'm Nancy Drew, and these are my friends George Fayne and Bess Marvin. In case you haven't noticed, Bess is a whiz with machines."

"Really? I'd never know *that,*" Ed said playfully, but then his expression grew serious as he studied my face. I shifted my gaze, uncomfortable under his intense scrutiny. Was there something wrong with me? Maybe leftover blueberries on my teeth, from that breakfast on the plane?

My thoughts were interrupted by the arrival of another cable car. We climbed aboard—this time on the outside platform. "Hold on tight, girls," Ed advised as the cable car lurched up the hill.

"This ride is awesome!" George exclaimed. I had to agree. I clutched the pole for support as we climbed upward. The higher we were, the bigger the sky seemed, until it was spread out around us on all sides.

When we took a slight plunge, my stomach leaped into my throat.

"Wow!" a small girl next to me said as we rolled downhill.

"It's a little like a slow roller coaster," Bess shouted against the wind.

"At least we're going forward this time," George declared.

The next hill was even steeper. The city spread out below us, its white buildings sparkling in the sun. Patches of purple bougainvillea spilled over garden walls, and palm trees dotted the hilly streets with green. But what was most awesome was the bay, its sapphire-colored water like a treasure beckoning us toward it. It almost looked close enough to touch. To our left a graceful bridge leaped across the water, its reddish cables stark against the hazy blue sky, only to be lost mysteriously in a cloud of mist at the far end.

"The Golden Gate Bridge," George said reverently.

Bess sighed. "There's something magical about that bay. And the bridge. No wonder people love this city."

Five minutes later we hopped off the car near Fisherman's Wharf and waved good-bye to Ed and Harriet. "Why don't we buy tickets for our boat tour?" George suggested. "Then if there's enough time before the boat leaves, we can explore the wharf."

There was a five-minute wait for tickets—not bad at all—so we took our places on line. As the family in front of us bought theirs, I heard familiar voices behind us.

"Hi, Nancy." I whirled around. Ed's green eyes gleamed as he caught my surprised look. "Harriet and I wondered if you girls would like something warm to drink at a nearby café? Please, let us treat you."

"Indeed," Harriet said. "We could all use a soothing drink after that harrowing cable car ride."

Wait—since when did Harriet get so chatty? My friends and I exchanged bewildered looks. Hadn't we left these two back on the cable car bound for their home? Were they following us?

"I thought you two were heading home," George said. Trust George to give voice to my innermost thoughts.

"Right you are, George," Ed said jovially, "but I realized we were out of chocolates. I'm absolutely bereft with no chocolates in the house, and Ghirardelli Square is right over there." He nodded in the direction of an old-fashioned brick complex set back from the bay. "Do you girls know about the Ghirardelli Chocolate Factory? It's a San Francisco institution."

Bess perked up at the mention of chocolates. George and I weren't sorry to hear about them either.

The wind picked up off the bay, and Harriet shivered. "We spotted you girls in line, and you looked awfully cold," she said, speaking for herself. "The cafés at Ghirardelli have divine hot chocolate."

I said, "That sounds nice, except we're about to catch the next boat tour of the harbor."

"Oh, come on!" Ed pleaded. "It's only eleven in the morning. There's plenty of time left in the day. That boat ride only takes an hour."

Bess shrugged. "I wouldn't mind sampling some San Francisco hot chocolate. And the weather might get warmer by the time we finish."

"Very true, dear," Harriet said. "No need to put up with unnecessary discomfort while sightseeing. Just listening to a tour guide can be torture enough."

As we followed Ed and Harriet toward Ghirardelli Square, George bent her head toward me and whispered, "Can you believe Harriet called Bess dear? I mean, up till now she's been a tough nut to crack."

"Something's up with her," I muttered back. "Harriet went through a total personality morph in under half an hour—from giving us the silent treatment to being our best friend."

And no sooner were we sipping our hot chocolate in a toasty café that smelled of coffee and croissants, than Harriet pulled out the biggest surprise of the day. Swiveling her chair toward mine, she said, "Nancy Drew—famous teen detective, I presume?" Her silvery eyes glistened as she waited for my answer.

I'm pretty good at keeping my cool, and this time was no exception. Still, I needed a moment to think. I mean, how on earth did this woman know who I was?

I glanced at my friends. George shot Harriet a skeptical frown. Bess, her mouth full of hot chocolate, looked as if she'd forgotten how to swallow.

"I had no clue people would have heard of me in a city so far from River Heights," I replied.

"Nancy, your fame precedes you," Ed said. "Thousands of miles from River Heights, we've heard of your skills. They're that impressive."

"Thanks," I said. Wasn't Ed going a bit overboard in the flattery department? I could tell George thought so from the look she shot me.

"Where are you girls staying?" Ed asked.

"The Old Bay Mare. It's a hotel on Nob Hill," I answered. "Originally it was someone's Victorian house."

"Have you found any mysteries to solve yet?"

"No," I said. "See, I'm on vacation."

"Vacation hasn't stopped you before," Harriet said, her eyes boring into mine. How did she know that? I was beginning to tire of this strange couple's nosy questions.

"I understand Bess and George are your assistant spies," Ed said, winking at my friends.

In a low, conspiratorial tone, Harriet asked, "Bess, can you describe the scariest situation you've experienced while helping Nancy?"

Bess squirmed in her seat. Instead of answering Harriet, she picked up the fortune cookie that came with her hot chocolate and inspected the message inside.

Bess's face whitened instantly—matching the whipped cream left in her cup—and the fortune dropped from her fingers. I picked it up off the floor before Harriet could grab it.

BEWARE OF NEW ACQUAINTANCES, the fortune advised. THEY MAY BE OLDER, BUT THEY ARE NOT ALWAYS WISER.

3

Stalkers

Thank you so much for our drinks," Bess said, pushing back her chair. "But we should definitely get going."

"Oh, but what's the rush?" Ed asked, grabbing the arm of her chair. "We're barely getting acquainted. Anyway," he added, offering us a plate of croissants, "Nancy and George aren't finished yet."

"Yes, we are," I said, catching Bess's pleading expression. Ed and Harriet were pummeling us with questions, and I didn't blame Bess for wanting to leave. George's face lit up at the sight of the croissants, but she'd have been less excited had she seen that creepy fortune.

Not that I believe in that stuff. Fortune or not, I'd had enough of Ed and Harriet to last me the rest of my vacation. I was beginning to feel as if they were behind the scenes of a strange dream I was having, like puppet masters.

"No thanks on the croissants," I said, trying my best to sound polite. "We had a big breakfast on the plane, and I want to save room for lunch after the boat ride."

George downed the rest of her hot chocolate in one gulp, then pushed back her chair. "I'm ready to leave anytime. I mean, look at this amazing weather. We don't want to miss it. Bess says it can change in a flash."

"It'll change when the fog rolls in from the Pacific Ocean late in the afternoon," Ed explained. "You girls have plenty of time to enjoy this lovely day, even if you linger here awhile longer."

I gathered the small backpack holding my camera, binoculars, and guidebook from under my chair. "Well, we'd better get in the ticket line so we won't miss the next boat."

After saying good-bye to Ed and Harriet politely but firmly, we hurried down to the wharf to buy tickets. Ten minutes later we were sitting on the prow of the small tour boat, speeding away from the dock into the bright blue bay. The wind was brisk, whipping my shoulder-length strawberry-blond hair around my face so that I could hardly see. George's short hair never troubles her, and she happily put her face up to the breeze like a puppy near an open car window. I tied my hair back in a band. Ditto for Bess.

Then Bess told George about her fortune. "It's as if it was an omen or something," she added. "That's why I wanted to leave. Ed and Harriet were spooking me."

With my back to the wind for shelter, I showed George the fortune. "I totally understand, Bess," George told her cousin reassuringly. "Not that I believe in fortunes, but Ed and Harriet's questions were getting nosier by the second. You don't have to justify leaving for my sake. It's great just to be on this boat."

"Thanks, George," Bess said, and grinned. One of Bess's most endearing qualities is that she's doesn't like to be a party pooper. The thought of pulling George or me away from a fun time would distress her deeply. Luckily Ed and Harriet weren't exactly our idea of fun.

Speaking through a megaphone, the tour guide told us about Alcatraz as we approached it. This tiny island in the middle of San Francisco Bay used to be a maximum-security prison. I could see why. Even if you escaped your cell, how would you get off the island? The bay is ice cold and choppy.

Slowly we approached the Golden Gate Bridge,

which soared over the water separating the bay from the Pacific Ocean. Beyond the bridge I could see the ocean, blue and sparkling. The horizon was a soft blue-violet, hinting of the fog to come. Behind us the city glittered jauntily on the hills above the bay.

After the boat ride we strolled through the chocolate store at Ghirardelli Square. I'd forgotten about Ed and Harriet during the boat ride, but the chocolates suddenly reminded me of them. I did my best to squash that memory for good.

A box of chocolates might help. We each bought one for ourselves and several more for our families back home. Hannah Gruen, housekeeper extraordinaire for Dad and me since my mother died years ago, loves chocolates, and Dad wouldn't turn down a box either.

Bess kept eyeing the other customers, as if she expected Ed and Harriet to appear any moment—but fortunately they didn't. "I'm starving!" I announced. "Are you two ready for lunch?"

"Let's go eat in Chinatown," George suggested. "My guidebook says it's a must-see."

"And a must-*shop*," Bess said happily, hailing a cab by the curb. "San Francisco's Chinatown is famous for its exotic stores—and architecture!"

After sharing a plate of delicious dim sum and spicy crabs, we poked around the shops overflowing with wares fresh from the Far East. Bess bought a parasol and some glittery slippers. George bought some batteries for her portable CD player. I found a small jade dragon figurine to give to Dad, a memento of the trip. But despite the many fun distractions around us, Bess kept glancing over her shoulder, as if she was scouting for stalkers. I couldn't help doing the same.

As we were returning to the Old Bay Mare loaded with shopping bags, I wondered how the cable car driver was doing—if he was okay. So I called the hospital to check on his condition, pretending I was a worried relative. Sure enough, he'd had a heart attack, but his doctors expected him to make a full recovery.

At sunset, after a rest and a shower, Bess, George, and I decided to get sodas at the Sky High, the famous restaurant in the penthouse of the ultra chichi Luke Jenkins Hotel up the street.

As usual George grumbled about dressing up. I'm not obsessed with clothes either, especially when I'm on the trail of a mystery. But since I had no mystery to focus on, I was perfectly happy to dress up for a big occasion: our first night out in San Francisco.

"Nancy, you look awesome," Bess said as she zipped up the back of my black scoop-neck silk dress. "George, you too."

George grinned. "Thanks, Bess. You promise you're not just being nice?"

Bess arched a brow, eyeing George's khaki slacks and white blouse. "I'm not so nice that I'd compliment your outfit if I didn't mean it. Your clothes are amazingly pressed, George. How did that happen inside that old backpack of yours?"

"Chalk it up to the Fayne folding technique. Here, Nancy, let me help you with your necklace." George took my necklace out of my hands and secured it around my neck. "Bess," George added, with a critical glance at Bess's high-heeled sandals, "are you really going to wear those things up that monster hill? You'll break your ankle."

"I'm a pro at walking in heels," Bess proclaimed. "But maybe a cable car goes by the hotel, so I won't need to show off my talent! Let's get directions to the Luke from the hotel clerk."

Unfortunately the cable car was packed (as usual), so we had to walk. But a mere fifteen minutes later we were sitting in the Sky High, sipping ginger ales and munching on baskets of chips and pretzels. Bess rubbed her ankle. "I guess you were right, George," she confessed. "I've got blisters, thanks to these shoes. Still, I am sooo glad to be here. This view is awesome, and the ginger ales aren't bad either."

Bess was right, especially about the view. As we

relaxed on a sofa facing a huge picture window, the lights of the city twinkled below us, and beyond them, the Golden Gate Bridge arched gracefully across the bay. Suddenly a fog rolled swiftly in from the ocean. It was as if we were drifting on a cloud island cut off from the rest of the world, except for a few light halos glowing faintly through the mist.

"Nancy?!" cried a woman behind me.

I started, then turned cautiously around. For once I fervently hoped my gut instinct was wrong.

It wasn't. Harriet grinned triumphantly down on us, looking as if she somehow knew we'd be here.

What luck.

A Missing Friend

Hello, Harriet," I said. My eyes met hers, which were as gray and mysterious as the fog outside. I fought to keep my wits about me as coolly as she kept hers. "What a coincidence meeting you again. Where's Ed?"

"Making a dinner reservation," she said as a tall figure emerged from the line of people waiting for tables. "And it's really not a coincidence running into you here."

I caught my friends' puzzled expressions. Their thoughts were pretty obvious. Why were Ed and Harriet stalking us? Bess's eyes were as wide as San Francisco Bay. George just rolled hers.

"Hello, girls," Ed said, walking up to join us. "Good to see you again."

"So why isn't it a coincidence running into us here?" George asked, getting right to the point as usual.

"Do you girls mind if I sit down?" Ed asked, plunking himself on the sofa between me and George. Harriet settled herself comfortably in an armchair next to Bess's, reminding me of a lazy cat sure of its quarry.

"Isn't this restaurant lovely?" Ed commented. "I haven't been here for years."

"It's popular with tourists," George said, "just like the cable cars."

"I don't mind doing touristy things once in a while," Ed declared. "Teaches me to appreciate the city. It would be a shame to take this unique metropolis for granted."

"But why did you come *tonight*?" George pressed. "To find us? *We* didn't know we'd be here till after we last saw you. How could you?"

"Don't worry, George, Harriet and I aren't psychic," Ed said with a chuckle. "We specifically came to find you girls, and we'd been told where you were. That's why Harriet said running into you was no coincidence."

The silence that greeted Ed's pronouncement made him chuckle louder. Then he slapped George and me on our backs with both hands.

I cringed. This guy belonged in a frat house, not at a fancy restaurant. His boisterous personality was almost as obnoxious as Harriet's proud silent one. "Who told you we were here?" I asked as calmly as I could.

Harriet laughed mischievously, a strange tinkling sound in the hushed room. "We called the Old Bay Mare looking for you," she explained, "and the clerk at the front desk made an educated guess. Don't you remember you'd asked him the way?"

Finally, a direct answer. And I wasn't surprised that Harriet was the one to give it.

But why were Harriet and Ed acting so cagey about telling us *why* they'd come? When I asked Harriet, she changed the subject. When I asked Ed, he told me to be patient.

So I decided to follow Ed's advice: I sat back and listened to them chat about their lives in San Francisco.

Finally my patience was rewarded. Even Ed ran out of chitchat after a lengthy yarn about cat fights in his backyard, and the conversation sputtered to an awkward silence.

"So you wonder why we came here to find you, Nancy?" Harriet asked.

"Well, yeah!" I said. "You've both gone to lots of trouble tracking us down—both here and at Fisherman's Wharf. I didn't think you were truly interested in getting hot cocoa or talking about cats."

"No, we weren't," Harriet agreed, "and your candid words have given me courage, Nancy."

"What my wife means," Ed said, cutting in, "is that we were reluctant to disturb your vacation by bringing up this mystery we have on our hands. So we beat around the bush, hoping to find a considerate moment to broach the subject."

"We really don't want to bother you," Harriet echoed. "You *are* on vacation, after all."

If only they'd known: The detective in me never takes a break. But most people don't realize how passionate I am about mysteries. How could they? "Don't worry about my vacation," I said. "As far as I'm concerned, a mystery would only make it better."

"Thanks, Nancy," Harriet said, "but George and Bess might like some time off." She shot a knowing glance at my friends, who kept their eyes fixed on me. I smiled. Maybe George and Bess agreed with Harriet, but they were way too supportive of me to tell her they'd prefer a vacation free of chasing dangerous criminals.

"So tell us about the mystery," I suggested. "Then we can decide whether we want to help."

Bess leaned toward me and mumbled, "I was hoping this vacation would be different. Obviously I hoped too soon."

Ed regarded his wife fondly. "Why don't you explain our mystery, Harriet?" he suggested. "You have a gift with words. You get to the point sooner than I do."

Preening, Harriet squared her shoulders. "You see, Nancy," she began, "Ed and I have a good friend named Mildred. She's a darling person in her mid-seventies. I don't know why anyone would want to hurt her, but the long and short of it is, she's disappeared."

"Disappeared! Does she live in San Francisco?" I asked.

"Indeed she does. But she disappeared on her way to Hawaii. Oh, the whole thing is so strange!" Harriet frowned, the first time a hint of emotion had crossed her face.

"But how do you disappear on an airplane?" Bess asked.

"We don't know whether she disappeared on the plane or later," Ed said. "Probably later. Because you're exactly right, Bess—disappearing on a plane just isn't possible."

"Actually, we know that Mildred got on the plane, because we checked with the airline. So she must have disappeared in Honolulu," Harriet added.

"She was traveling by herself?" I asked.

Harriet nodded. "Mildred is a mystery writer, and

the plot of her new book involves Hawaiian legends. She left two days ago to research myths about the Night Marchers. They're ghostly warriors, I believe."

"Ghostly warriors?" Bess echoed, her blue eyes wide. I could tell she was warming to the mystery.

Ed grabbed a handful of chips. "You see, girls," he said, munching away, "Harriet and I are mystery-book publishers, and Mildred is one of our writers. She's also a friend, of course. We have her new book under contract, and in her outline for it she describes these ghostly warriors. From what I remember, they carry torches and march at night along old battle-grounds. They allow no disturbances from mortals. In fact, if you look them in the eye or stand in their way, legend has it you'll die."

"You mean, you'll just drop dead?" Bess asked, horrified.

"Sometimes," Ed said. "Or else you'll waste away. The ghosts pound drums and chant as they march along. Their feet never touch the ground."

"Weird!" Bess declared. "Let's hope Mildred didn't run into any Night Marchers."

"They're legends, Bess," Ed said firmly. "Mildred doesn't believe in them, and neither do I. And neither should you girls."

"Sounds like an unusual topic for a mystery book," George said. "I can see why Mildred wanted to go to Hawaii to research it. Especially if she hoped to interview people who claim they've seen the ghosts. And the libraries and bookstores there must have lots of info about local myths that would be hard to find anywhere else."

Harriet looked thoughtful. "Mildred also wanted to see where the ghosts supposedly march, just to get the right atmosphere for her book. It's important for a mystery to have a realistic setting. Details are crucial."

"Do you know the name of the hotel where Mildred was planning to stay?" I asked.

"She didn't book a hotel," Ed said. "Mildred had arranged to stay with her cousin in Honolulu before traveling to Maui for a few extra days of research. But she never showed up. Her cousin called earlier today to tell us the news. I got the call on my cell phone shortly after you girls had left the cable car."

"That's why we tracked you down at Fisherman's Wharf—to ask for your help," Harriet explained. "But we chickened out. I mean, it *is* your vacation."

"We'd be happy to give you advice anytime," I said, "and I could easily make some phone calls. But what else could we do from so far away?"

Ed's and Harriet's eyes met before glancing back at me. Harriet smoothed her gray hair, elegantly braided in a French twist, with trembling fingers.

"You see, Nancy," she said, "Ed and I bought tickets for Hawaii on a flight tomorrow morning, hoping to track down our friend. But business has interfered. A cover-art disaster on one of our biggest books for next year! Unfortunately we have to stay in town."

Ed leaned forward. "So," he said, "would you girls care to take our places, all expenses paid?"

5

New Adventures

H awaii?" **Bess cried. "Free** of charge?"

Exactly my thoughts. I was floored. But I immediately spotted problems with this proposal, awesome though it was. First, there were only two of Ed and Harriet, so would George or Bess have to draw straws for the cargo hold? I decided right away that I wouldn't go without both my friends. Choosing between them would be wrong. Second, what about the rest of our vacation in San Francisco? Could I persuade my friends to abandon it for Hawaii? Judging by Bess's reaction, it might not be too hard.

Or maybe it would. Frowning, George said, "That's incredibly generous of you, but we've barely seen any of San Francisco. We were looking forward to spending more time here. At least I was."

"You can always come back for another visit," Ed said. "It's a very welcoming place."

"But what about the third plane ticket?" I asked. "There are two of you and three of us."

"We've already bought another ticket for the third one of your group, whoever she may be," Ed said with a playful grin. "So all three of you girls can go. We won't make you fight over plane seats as if they were musical chairs."

My jaw dropped. They'd actually bought an extra ticket for us? How generous. But that brought me to my third problem with this trip: Ed and Harriet *themselves*. There was no getting around the fact that we didn't know this couple from Adam. Could we trust them? And then there was the fourth: why did they want me to investigate, instead of a professional?

"I don't see how we can accept this offer," Bess declared. "You're being way too generous."

Ed tucked his chin down, looking embarrassed. "Ah, well, Bess, we really care a lot about Mildred, and we're determined to find her. And Harriet and I think that you girls are up to the job. If anyone can find her, Nancy Drew can."

"After all, Bess, we're not offering you the tickets so you can lie on the beach," Harriet said gruffly. "We expect results. That is, if Mildred is still . . . well, if she's still all right."

36

A chill ran through me as I took in Harriet's unspoken meaning. But really, why wouldn't Mildred be okay? Maybe she'd decided to run away from her old life. Or maybe she'd hurt her head in the airport and had amnesia. There were so many possibilities for what might have happened to Mildred that my head was spinning. No reason to assume up front that she'd been a victim of foul play.

"I'm really impressed by how much you care about Mildred," I said. "Buying tickets all the way to Hawaii to find her. She must be a special person. Can you tell us a little bit about her?"

Ed's green eyes twinkled. "Gladly. Mildred is in her seventies and has gray hair and sharp, sparkly brown eyes. She's smart, fun, and lively, but the best thing about her is her free-spirited nature. She's never afraid to seek adventure, never afraid to speak her mind."

"And she's always cheerful," Harriet added. "Innocent, too, even though her books are action packed and filled with all sorts of mayhem and crime."

Ed said, "She's also pretty absentminded. That's why we want to make sure she's okay."

My mind was packed with images of a sweet but feisty Mildred. I could see why Ed and Harriet wanted to find her. But Ed and Harriet were pretty eccentric. Could they have some other sneaky reason for sending us so far away to find their friend? Like wanting to get us out of town so I wouldn't catch wind of a crime they were involved with here?

Did Mildred even exist?

Ed and Harriet leaned toward me, their drinks forgotten on the table. "Um, could I see your business card first?" I asked.

Ed drew a small white card out of his wallet and handed it to me. "We're legit, I promise," he said.

I'd heard that line before. I studied the card. It listed Ed's and Harriet's names and the name of their publishing firm, Crime Time Books, plus the phone number, address, and Web site underneath. A small black mask—the firm's logo—appeared in the bottom right corner. So far, so good. Maybe they were telling the truth. I wanted to believe them.

Of course, I'm naturally susceptible to mysteries. And a mystery in Hawaii? I mean, how awesome was that? It was probably the one vacation spot on earth more tempting than San Francisco.

But I knew better than to fall for wishful thinking. Before we accepted this wild invitation, I had to check this couple out.

I met Ed's hopeful gaze, while Harriet averted her eyes. Could she actually be worried we'd say no? "Well, your offer is amazing," I said. "But I'll have to think about it. Can I get back to you later tonight?"

Ed's eyes clouded over, and he shook his head firmly. "I'm afraid not, Nancy. We need an answer now. There's no time to wait. The plane leaves tomorrow morning."

"It's now or never," Harriet declared.

"Okay, you'll have to excuse me for a moment," I said, "uh . . . to the ladies' room." Thank goodness for that old excuse. Where would my snooping career be without it?

"I'm coming too, Nancy," Bess said, grabbing her handbag. George shot us a reproachful look as we left her alone with Ed and Harriet.

Once out of their view, Bess and I slipped into an elevator bound for the lobby. "I'd really like to believe them," I said as we filed into the huge ornate room with its glittering chandeliers. "But I know better than to easily accept candy from strangers."

"You're right, Nancy," Bess agreed. "A free trip sounds too good to be true."

"Let's do some research." I scanned the lobby and soon found what I wanted: a discreet row of computers for guests to use. "I'll check out the Crime Time Books Web site on one of the computers over there."

"What can I do?"

"Hmm. It's not too late to call some of the chain bookstores. Maybe you could verify that Crime Time Books isn't some shady operation?"

"Consider it done," Bess said brightly, removing her cell phone from her purse.

I strolled over to an unoccupied computer terminal. A few seconds later I'd brought up the Web site of Crime Time Books. Sure enough, the firm seemed legitimate. Names, addresses, and upcoming books were prominently displayed. Mildred's book didn't seem to be scheduled yet, but it was mentioned in a column of upcoming titles. Unless the whole Web site was a scam, Ed and Harriet's business obviously existed.

"I called two stores," Bess said at my shoulder as I logged off, "and both of them praised Crime Time Books. The company always ships its books on time. Some of its authors are really popular." Bess cocked her head. "So, are you on that plane tomorrow, Nancy?"

"What do you mean, 'you'? Aren't you coming?"

Bess frowned. "Maybe."

"I'll take that as a yes."

"Okay," Bess said, sounding unconvinced. "But I'll want to at least try to get in a teeny bit of beach time."

We returned to the lounge upstairs, where the other three were digging into a new basket of chips. "What took you guys so long?" George asked.

Harriet looked at me suspiciously. She knew we'd been checking her out.

"So where can I buy some tropical weather clothes?" I asked.

Ed guffawed, slapping the table. Harriet glared at him with critical eyes, but then she looked at me and smiled broadly, her face full of relief. My detective instincts couldn't spot the slightest bit of insincerity in her at all. At least not on the surface.

"So we can count on you, Nancy?" Harriet asked gratefully. "And on Bess and George, too?"

I nodded.

Back at the Old Bay Mare, after we'd taken care of travel plans and grabbed a bite to eat at the Luke courtesy of Ed and Harriet, Bess turned to George and me with a troubled expression. "I don't know, guys," she said, closing the door to our room behind us. "I'm really not sure I want to go to Hawaii."

"What?" George said. "But Ed and Harriet bought your ticket. You told them you'd go. I mean, they *paid* for it."

"Yeah, well, they did that before they found out if any of us were actually going," Bess retorted. "They were willing to take the risk of getting stuck with it."

"True," I said, "but why are you suddenly getting cold feet, Bess? You seemed okay during dinner."

Bess bit her lip. "Actually, I wasn't. I thought maybe I'd feel better about the trip once I got used to the idea of it. But that hasn't happened yet, and I doubt it will by tomorrow morning."

"So what's bothering you?" George asked. "You love beach vacations, Bess. I'm surprised."

"This won't be a vacation," Bess replied. She threw up her hands. "It's just that Ed and Harriet still seem weird, okay? I know we checked them out and they're supposedly legit, but . . ." Bess paused, then glanced at George and me sheepishly. "If you have to know, I'm still creeped out by that fortune cookie."

"Enough to turn down this trip?" I asked. "What would you do instead?"

Bess smiled. "I don't know. Wait for you and George to come back to San Francisco, maybe?"

"You mean you'd hang here with Ed and Harriet lurking around?" George said in a shocked voice. "Your fortune warned you about them."

She shot me a smirk.

Bess shivered. "Well, when you put it like that, George, maybe I should come along."

"Think of all the adventures we've had together, Bess," I said. "Don't you want to share this one too? And don't worry about Ed and Harriet. First, we checked them out, and they're okay. Second, they'll be in San Francisco, thousands of miles from Hawaii! And the weather in Hawaii will be awesome. We'll be totally fine."

"The fun is just starting, Bess," George added.

"Only it's going to be in Hawaii instead of San Francisco. Who knew?"

Bess grinned. "Okay, guys, I'm convinced. I was always worried about poor Mildred. Someone's got to find her, it's true. Why shouldn't it be us?"

After quick calls to our families informing them of our unscheduled detour, we were off. We disembarked from the plane into a hot sunny morning at the Honolulu airport. Going from brisk San Francisco to hot Hawaii sure was a pleasant shock. Residents in shorts and tank tops greeted arriving passengers by showering them with leis, and the heavy scent of tropical flowers wafted through the taxi pickup area.

"Ah, the smell of the South Seas!" Bess exclaimed, sniffing the air as we piled inside a cab. "I feel as if I'm in a different country—the flowers and trees are so lush."

Bess was right. In addition to palm trees too numerous to count, gardens filled with giant red and orange flowers decorated the roads leading from the airport. "So Honolulu is the capital of Hawaii, huh?" George said. "And it's on the island of Oahu?"

"Yup," I said, remembering sixth-grade history class when we'd studied the states. "There are a bunch of islands that make up the state of Hawaii,

43

including one actually named Hawaii."

"Nicknamed the Big Island," the cab driver declared. "We also nickname the continental US the Mainland. Anyway, girls, aloha! That's the Hawaiian greeting. Where to?"

I gave him the address of Mildred's cousin, Eliza Bingham, who had invited us to stay with her while we searched for Mildred. Toward the end of our dinner last night with Ed and Harriet, Ed had called Eliza on his cell phone just to check in. There had still been no word of Mildred's whereabouts, so Ed and Harriet had given us the thumbs-up to go forward with our investigation. That involved talking briefly to Eliza.

Eliza had sounded nice, but spacey, on the phone. Maybe she was so worried about Mildred that her mind couldn't focus. But she was sweet to let us stay with her, seeing as we were perfect strangers.

We wove our way to the top of a hill overlooking Honolulu. The Pacific Ocean spread out below us, stretching as far as the eye could see and making me feel microscopic in comparison. The giant green crater of the extinct volcano Diamond Head lurked like a slumbering dragon on the edge of Honolulu, between us and the sea.

Soon we arrived at Eliza's house, a trim red ranch house surrounded by banana trees. We paid the cab driver, collected our luggage, then rang the front bell. Bess and George looked exhausted from the distance we'd traveled since River Heights, but I felt fine, eager to track down Mildred.

The door swung open, and a woman stepped outside to greet us. She was probably in her midforties and gorgeous, with long thick honey blond hair and bluish green, sparkling eyes. But those qualities were not what caught my eye. The huge red, green, and blue parrot that sat on her shoulder did. He looked at me fiercely, then squawked, "She's cool!"

"Is he talking about me or you?" I asked, grinning.

"Me, of course!" the woman answered. "He likes to whisper sweet nothings into my ear."

"Whisper?" Bess said. "I'm surprised you can still hear."

The woman laughed. "Come in, girls. As you've no doubt guessed, I'm Eliza Bingham, Mildred's cousin, and this big bird here is Jack."

"Don't leave me!" Jack cut in as we followed Eliza into the spacious front room that served as a living area.

"Nancy, George, and Bess, I presume?" Eliza went on, ignoring the parrot and pointing to each of us with the right guesses. "By the way, don't mind Jack. He always interrupts. Rudeness is second nature to him."

45

"She's my pal!" Jack proclaimed.

"You're a horrible pest," Eliza scolded, holding out two fingers for Jack to hop up on. "You go directly to jail without passing Go so I can greet my new guests." Eliza shoved Jack into an enormous white cage on a nearby table.

My gaze roamed the room. There were birdcages everywhere with colorful birds of all different sizes and shapes inside them. A few birds fluttered freely around the room, landing on Eliza's head for brief moments before soaring away. "Let's go out to the lanai and talk," Eliza suggested, pointing toward a screened porch chock-full with tropical plants of every size and description in assorted pots. "*Lanai* is Hawaiian for 'porch,'" she added.

We settled ourselves on comfortable chairs overlooking Diamond Head while Eliza brought us refreshing glasses of pineapple juice and a giant bowl of macadamia nuts, a rich Hawaiian treat. Several birds flapped overhead before settling on nearby branches. "So what do you think happened to Mildred?" I asked, getting right to the point.

Eliza's face clouded over. "I don't know. I'm beside myself with worry. I've checked all the hospitals, but no luck. She must have disappeared at the airport."

Strange—she didn't seem all that beside herself. "What makes you think that?"

"Well, she was definitely on the plane. We're certain from airline records and from witnesses. The person she sat next to—his name is Jamey Ching—claims she got off and disappeared into the crowd of arriving passengers. He was the last person we know of who saw her."

"Was she planning to come straight to your house?"

"Yes. I took the morning off from work to meet her, just as I'm doing now for you. It's no trouble, of course," she added hastily.

"Do you know if she'd rented a car?" Bess asked.

"She was planning to take a taxi here from the airport. I'd told her she could borrow my extra car once she arrived. By the way, my extra car is at your disposal, Nancy. It's a red sedan."

"Thanks, Eliza. I may take you up on your offer," I said gratefully. "So the police know that Mildred is missing, right?"

For a moment Eliza was distracted by two small birds that landed on her juice glass to inspect its contents. "Of course I called the police, Nancy," Eliza said in a slightly annoyed tone, "but they seemed to shrug off my worries. They're not taking the case seriously enough."

She sighed. Then, with a bird perched on each shoulder, Eliza started to tell us how much she adored Mildred, a much older cousin. "Mildred was so sweet to me when I was little. Even now she's so supportive, so generous. Do you know that she's twenty-eight years older than I am? But our age difference never got in the way of our relationship. I always felt I could tell her anything. If anything bad has happened to her"—Eliza's voice cracked—"I'd feel so alone," she added, shaking her head.

"Are you an only child?" Bess asked sympathetically.

"I am," Eliza said. "And so is Mildred. Our parents are both dead, which is kind of obvious in Mildred's case since she's in her seventies. After my parents died, we only had each other."

"But what could have happened to her?" George asked, looking baffled. "Could someone really disappear into thin air between the airport and here?"

"Apparently so," Eliza said. No one spoke as Eliza's words hung in the air. Then she set her juice glass on an end table. "Girls, I've got to get going. I told my boss I'd be in after lunch."

"Where do you work?" Bess asked.

"I'm a botany researcher at a cosmetics company in downtown Honolulu. The work is intense, but my boss understands that Mildred takes priority. Unfortunately I don't think he'll feel that way forever, so I'm glad you've arrived, Nancy, to help me search.

Anyway, girls, please make yourselves comfortable—
I'll be back by six. Oh, and the keys to my sedan are
on the kitchen table. Feel free to use it whenever you
like."

"Thanks, Eliza," I said. "We'll get to work finding
Mildred pronto."

The moment the door closed behind Eliza, Bess
flopped down on the lanai sofa. "I'm sorry to be such
a wimp, guys, but I've got jet lag big-time. A quick nap
will fix me up so I can be a sharper assistant sleuth."

"Snooze all you want, Bess," I said. "Meanwhile,
George and I will search the house."

George looked surprised. "Hey, Nancy, do you
suspect Eliza?"

"I might," I said as we moved into the living room
so Bess could sleep. "We only have Eliza's word that
Mildred is missing. What if she picked her up at the
airport and is holding her hostage or something?"

"A long shot," George said dubiously.

"Sure, but as a detective, I can't take anything for
granted, even Eliza's honesty. So you search Eliza's
bedroom while I poke around in here." I hated to
rummage in this seemingly nice woman's things—
but the case called for it.

Fortunately Eliza's house was small, and except for
the birds and plants, free of clutter, too. Her bedroom, our guest room, a sunny kitchen, and the lanai

opened off the spacious living room, and a garage and storage basement provided extra space. Only five minutes into the search, George let out a cry of excitement from Eliza's bedroom. "Nancy, check this out!"

Standing outside Eliza's closet, George held up a pink sleeveless dress with a pattern of black-and-white geometrical designs. "Take a look," she added, pointing at the back tag. "Mildred must have been here after all. Eliza lied to us."

I peered at the dress. Sure enough, Mildred's name appeared there in black permanent marker— probably for easy identification at the dry cleaner's. But did that mean Eliza was a liar? I scanned the room, looking for more clues. "Have you searched the drawers?" I asked.

"Just the dresser drawers. I haven't checked the night table yet."

The one drawer in the night table was all I needed. Inside, among a jumble of pens and receipts, lay a green velvet diary. My hands shook with excitement as I pulled it out and opened to a random page.

Dated thirty years ago, the entry didn't describe the friendly relationship Eliza claimed she had with Mildred. "Mildred is an annoying snob," Eliza had written in large neat letters, with happy faces drawn inside the o's. "Whenever she comes to visit us, she's a horrible know-it-all. And my parents LOVE her even though she bosses me around like I'm still a kid. She doesn't seem to get that I'm fifteen years old! Sometimes I wish she'd just vanish. And I mean *off the face of the earth!*"

The front door slammed, and a loud voice squawked, "She's back!"

6

Tropical Terror

George and I jumped at least five feet. "It's Jack!" I cried, catching George's alarmed gaze.

"Announcing *Eliza*!" George whispered.

I quickly stuffed Eliza's diary back in the drawer before hurrying into the living room, with George at my heels.

But the person we saw there was a different blond, not Eliza.

"Bess! You scared the heck out of us," George scolded.

Bess stood by the front door, a puzzled look in her sleepy blue eyes. "What are you talking about, George? I scared *you*?"

"We thought you were Eliza," George explained breathlessly. "Jack screamed that she was back, and we were snooping around in her room. Something tells me she wouldn't like that."

"I went outside for a walk after my power nap—I just needed a few minutes," Bess said. "When I came back in, Jack announced that I was back."

I shot Jack an annoyed look. His beady eyes stared at me coldly, as if I was a worm.

George and I told Bess about the dress and the diary. "Good clues," she declared. "You guys are on a roll. Let's hunt for more."

We slipped back into Eliza's room. Once more I took out the diary and leafed through more entries, but everything inside was typical girl stuff from decades ago. Nothing seemed to relate to the present time. I replaced it in the drawer and searched the rest of the house for more clues. Other than the dress, we found no hints of Mildred's presence or signs of where she might be. After putting everything back in its place, I slumped down in an armchair by the living-room phone and picked up the receiver.

"I'm going to call the police and get an update," I announced. "If they have a lead, we might as well follow it too."

But after a brief phone conversation with Officer Pamela Kona, I felt totally let down. The police had no more information than we did—unless they just weren't telling me about it. Eliza was right. The police didn't seem terribly concerned about Mildred. Officer Kona assured me that she and her fellow officers were on the case, but until more clues popped up, there wasn't much they could do.

I know better. There's *always* a way to find more clues if you look hard enough—and I was determined to find Mildred.

Two seconds after I'd hung up the phone, it rang. My friends and I started, then traded looks as I answered it.

"Hi, it's Eliza. Is this Nancy?"

"Yes. Hi, Eliza."

"How would you girls like to join me for some fresh seafood tonight when I finish work—my treat? I'll give you directions to the Purple Porpoise." I jotted them down, then thanked her for her invitation before hanging up. Eliza was such a generous, welcoming person that I hated to suspect her. But I immediately thought of the dress and the diary, so I set aside my friendly feelings. Finding Mildred had to come first. If I let emotion cloud my judgment, we'd never get anywhere in this case.

I told Bess and George that Eliza wanted to treat us to dinner. "Excellent! But what'll we do between now and then?" Bess wondered.

"What about something Hawaiian like snorkeling or wind surfing?" George suggested. "I mean, we've exhausted all the clues in this house, at least for now. We might as well treat ourselves to some fun while we have the chance."

I wasn't crazy about suspending our search, but George was right. Until we could ask Eliza about the dress, we might as well go snorkeling. After all, Hawaii was famous for great water sports, and exercise might sharpen my mind.

The weather was perfect, and once on the beach at Hanauma Bay just outside Honolulu, we waded into the crystal blue water in our rented flippers and masks.

Diving under the gentle surface of the bay, we were transported to another world. Tropical fish of every color and variety darted around the reef. Sunlight slanted through the water, highlighting the brilliant oranges, yellows, blues, and purples of the zillions of sea creatures that lived and fed there. We returned to Eliza's house feeling more relaxed and refreshed. After showering and dressing, we hopped into Eliza's sedan and followed her directions to the Purple Porpoise.

Eliza arrived seconds ahead of us, and within an hour we were all seated at a quiet table under an outdoor thatched roof as the sun began to set over the beach. "I'd recommend the mahimahi," Eliza told us after we'd ordered our drinks. "That's a delicious white fish, native to Hawaii." She peered at the menu. "This recipe includes a special coconut lime sauce. Yum!"

We all followed Eliza's suggestion and ordered mahimahi. After talking briefly about our snorkeling expedition that afternoon, I cut right to the chase. "I spoke with Officer Kona to ask if she had any new info on Mildred," I said. "And you were right, Eliza, the police don't seem that focused on her. But there's something else I want to ask you."

Eliza looked at me with her clear green eyes. My stomach knotted. She wasn't going to seem so friendly once I'd got to talking. And there was no way I dared bring up snooping in her diary. Finding Mildred's dress in Eliza's closet would be hard enough to explain.

"So what do you want to ask me, Nancy?" Eliza asked.

"There's this dress in your closet—pink with a black-and-white pattern," I said airily. "Well, I noticed Mildred's name on the tag. Could she have come to your house without you knowing?"

Eliza's eyes narrowed, and a chill came over her like a hailstorm in August. "Why were you were prying in my closet?" she asked coldly.

"Uh, I was looking for beach towels," I fudged. "You know, for snorkeling."

"And you checked the tags on every dress of mine?"

"Well, the dress dropped off the hook when I moved the hanger," I said hastily. "I thought there might be towels on the side shelves, and some of the clothes were covering them. Your dress fell on the floor by mistake, and naturally I didn't want to leave it there. And, naturally, I noticed Mildred's name on the tag when I hung the dress back up."

"Naturally," Eliza said. But her belligerent expression softened as doubt flickered through her eyes, and she added, "Well, okay, I guess that makes sense."

"So it looks like Mildred came to the house after all," I pressed. "Maybe when you were at work?"

My words hung in the air as Eliza calmed down. Like a bird pulling in its feathers but still keeping an eye out for cats, she began her explanation. "Mildred gave me that dress during a visit here five years ago. I really liked it, and I told her so. One evening after she'd worn it to a party, she tossed it to me in a burst of annoyance."

"A burst of annoyance?" Bess echoed.

"Mildred claimed the dress had grown too tight thanks to all the macadamia nuts I'd been feeding her on her trip. She was irritated that it didn't fit her anymore."

"She was generous to give it to you, Eliza," George said with a skeptical glance at our host. I could tell George didn't totally buy her story. For that matter, neither did I.

Eliza shrugged. "Mildred could barely wear it anymore. How generous is that?"

"But you two get along, don't you?" I asked, surprised at Eliza's critical tone.

"Of course. Why?" Eliza said. "Look, Nancy, if you don't believe me about the dress, get the police to dust my house for Mildred's fingerprints. You'll see that your suspicions are dead wrong. Mildred hasn't set foot in it for at least five years."

"Sorry," I said, feeling guilty for giving her the third degree. After all, we were her guests. "I really didn't mean to sound suspicious of you, Eliza. I'm just trying to follow leads, and I thought it was possible Mildred had come to your house. You have to admit you spend a lot of time at work. You might not have known she'd even been there."

"Like I told you, that dress is old," she said shortly.

"I believe you." Even though maybe I didn't. What choice did I have but to play along? Another awkward silence fell while we all concentrated on our dinners. I mean, how straight was Eliza being with us? What were her real feelings about Mildred now that they both were adults?

"Anyway," Eliza said after finishing her meal, "I think I know what happened to Mildred. The more I ponder this thing, the more I believe my theory is right."

"So, what do you think happened?" I asked.

"Something supernatural has abducted Mildred," Eliza said. "It's the only explanation."

As the waiters took our plates away, I searched her face. Was there a hint of a smile at the corners of her mouth? I couldn't tell. But she had to be joking.

"Yeah, right," George said, rolling her eyes.

"Don't mock me, George," Eliza said angrily. "I'm serious."

"Why don't you tell us what you mean by *supernatural,* Eliza?" I suggested. "But first, thanks so much for dinner. It was delicious."

"You're welcome," Eliza said as she signed the check. "Hey, why don't we go home and have dessert there? I baked a mango pie early this morning. And besides, I don't want other diners to overhear me talk about ghosts. They'll think I'm crazy."

By the time we got home, Eliza was Ms. Cheerful. I fervently hoped she'd forgotten her grudge so she wouldn't clam up and withhold information.

"Pie, anyone? I've got fresh whipped cream to go with it, and wonderful Hawaiian decaf coffee." Eliza whirled around her kitchen as she sliced the pie and set out the coffee. Then we followed her onto the lanai. With the lights of Honolulu sprinkled below us in the darkness, we dug into our dessert.

Bess's face lit up with the first bite. The pie was definitely delicious. "So, Eliza," I said after a comfortable silence, "what do you mean by Mildred disappearing thanks to something supernatural?"

Eliza's face hardened. "Nancy, please. It's late. I'm tired. Tomorrow is a work day for me. I honestly don't feel like talking right now, especially about Mildred. She's disappeared without a trace, and I'm having a really hard time with that."

I exchanged frustrated looks with Bess and George. "We're trying to help you find her, Eliza, and talking about the case helps," I said.

"Not now," Eliza said, her chin set. She stood up to collect the dishes. "Let's make sure you girls have clean sheets on your beds."

I sighed. Obviously Eliza wasn't budging.

"Eliza is like a chameleon," Bess declared as we climbed into twin beds and a cot in the spacious guest room. "You can never tell what her mood will be. She goes from friendly to aloof, then from mad to happy. I think she's hiding something."

"Yeah. Like Mildred?" George whispered before we all drifted into a troubled sleep.

A bell rang far away in a clock tower. I had to run through a long dark passage to stop it, but my legs wouldn't move. Something disastrous would happen if I didn't get there on time. Then I forced my legs to run, and I tumbled into a warm ocean made of cotton. The ringing stopped.

Something creaked, and my eyes flew open. I instantly remembered my dream. But how much time had passed since I'd dreamed it? I felt as if I'd spent hours in the cottony ocean, my mind stripped of memory and thought. My gaze rested on the glow-in-the-dark clock on the bedside table: 3:00 A.M.

A floorboard groaned outside the bedroom door. That must be the noise that woke me! I hopped out of bed. My bare feet were as stealthy as cat's paws as I tiptoed to the door and cracked it open.

I peeked out.

Jack, shrouded in his cage under a dark sheet, slept peacefully. But there was definitely someone there— a shadow loomed against the far wall. I stepped into the living room.

A long-haired figure in a sweater and white nightgown was wandering around, her delicate fingers lifting objects and putting them back down as if she was in a daze. She turned toward me, her eyes catching the moonlight.

Eliza!

I hurried up to her, then recoiled in shock. Her

nightgown was caked in mud—and what were those bloody scratches all over her face?

"I was out searching for Mildred," she whispered. "I barely escaped an army of ghosts."

The Haunted Message

An army of *ghosts*? **Who** was she kidding? I studied Eliza closely. She wore a gray sweatshirt over her gown, and hiking boots caked with red dirt. The scratches on her face were random zigzags, as if she'd been gouged by briars, not by knife-wielding ghosts. Did she really believe she'd been attacked by spirits?

"What do you mean, 'an army of ghosts'?" I asked her.

"I think my meaning is plain," she said through gritted teeth.

"Let me get you something to drink, Eliza," I suggested, moving into the kitchen.

I found some chamomile tea in one of Eliza's cabinets, and within minutes handed her a steaming cup. Then I gently washed off her face and dabbed it with peroxide before sitting down across from her at the kitchen table.

"I want to hear everything you did tonight, from start to finish."

"Oh, Nancy, I was so scared. Have you heard about the Night Marchers?" I nodded, and Eliza went on, "Well, I guess you know that Mildred came to Hawaii to research them. I'm sure Ed and Harriet told you about her book. Anyway, I think her disappearance has something to do with the research she's doing!"

Eliza's gloomy silence from earlier that evening had given way to a babble, which was fine by me. Maybe I would finally learn something from her. At this point I'd settle for any lead in the case, no matter how small. Mildred was out there somewhere, maybe cold, probably frightened. I doubted her old bones could take too much exposure. And she'd been missing for almost three days!

"You mean Mildred's research somehow caused her disappearance?" I asked.

In a barely audible voice, as if she was still frightened, Eliza answered. "See," she said, "the weather was nice when Mildred arrived at the airport, so I'm guessing she took a quick detour on her way here without telling anyone—except for the taxi driver, of course."

"A detour? But where would she go?"

"To this area near the Pali Highway where the Night Marchers congregate. That's where I saw them tonight! This place is minutes away from Honolulu, and Mildred often does things on the spur of the moment, so it's plausible."

"I guess that fits with what I've heard about her. Ed and Harriet told me she's a real free spirit."

"Free spirits run in the family, Nancy," Eliza declared. "Anyway, I think that Mildred went to this place and ran into ghosts."

"But it was daylight when she arrived," I said. "I thought the ghosts didn't come out till night. Otherwise they'd be called Day Marchers." I smirked.

"Don't joke, Nancy," Eliza said gravely. "These are dangerous spirits, and you should take them seriously. But you're right. Mildred arrived here in broad daylight when the Night Marchers shouldn't have been a bother."

I took a long look at Eliza's earnest face. Even with its marks, she was beautiful, like some damsel in distress from the middle ages. "You really do believe in the myth of the Night Marchers, Eliza," I said. "I don't think you're faking."

"Of course I believe in them, Nancy!" she cried in a wounded tone. "I told you I saw them."

"Okay, I believe that you believe in them. But I go

by evidence, not ghostly legends," I told her. "There's no way you can prove a legend."

"You'll have to take my word for it that the Night Marchers exist."

"Then show them to me. You mentioned the Pali Highway. Let's go there now!" I shot up from my chair.

Eliza gasped, splashing her tea on the table as she set it down. "Nancy, are you *crazy*? I can't possibly take you there now. It's way too dangerous! I barely escaped the Night Marchers already tonight. I'm not going to push my luck."

"Eliza, the situation is simple. How can you expect me to think that ghosts captured Mildred unless you can prove they exist?"

She looked at me pleadingly. "You just have to believe me."

"If these ghosts exist, then three thirty in the morning is the perfect time to prove it. You say they're out at night and you saw them."

Eliza looked like a ghost herself, her face was so pale. "Okay," she said reluctantly. "This hiking trail is near the Pali Highway. It was raining there earlier, but if it's stopped, I'll take you."

"Excellent!" I cried. I couldn't wait.

"Let's write a note to Bess and George," Eliza suggested. "We should tell them where we're going as a safety measure. They'll need to know where to locate our bodies after the Marchers are finished with us."

"I'm not planning to let the Marchers get me so easily," I said firmly. "But a note to George and Bess is a good idea, so they won't freak out if they wake in the night and find us missing." After dispatching the note, we threw on clothes and hiking boots, then hopped into Eliza's cute black convertible. The rain had stopped, so she happily put the top down, and soon we were speeding through the hushed streets of Honolulu, the only car in sight.

"The Pali Highway runs between Honolulu and the North Shore of Oahu," Eliza explained. We'd already left the city behind and were zooming down a narrow highway with high volcanic ridges rising on either side of us.

"I've heard about the North Shore from surfing movies," I mentioned.

"It's really popular with surfers, because of the giant waves rolling in from the north," Eliza declared. "And the North Shore is less developed than the Honolulu area."

We raced through a tunnel, and about a quarter of a mile later, Eliza slowed down and turned the car into a small rest area. "Here we are, Nancy. Are you sure you're up for this?"

"Positive." I climbed out of the car, and in the headlights I noticed a hiking trail snaking through heavy foliage on our left. Eliza turned off the ignition, and everything went dark.

A sudden burst of light made me blink. "Here, Nancy," Eliza said, handing me a flashlight and keeping another one for herself. "You'll need it."

"Thanks, Eliza. Are you ready?" But she was shaking so much that I wondered whether she could make it up the trail.

"I don't know if I'll ever be ready for this adventure. We're doomed, Nancy," she whispered in a small terrified voice. "Maybe you should go without me."

I had to cheer her on. I'd already resolved to go alone, but I didn't relish the prospect. "You came here by yourself earlier tonight, Eliza," I said in a chirpy, upbeat tone. "That was really brave. And this time you've got me for company. So if you could tough it out before, things will be much easier this time."

Eliza shot me a dubious look. Her timid manner was so different from the confident woman who'd greeted us upon our arrival from the airport earlier.

"Plus I need you to show me exactly where you saw those ghosts," I added.

She took a deep breath. "Okay, Nancy. I'd never forgive myself if I abandoned you to those dreadful apparitions. But I sure am glad that we left Bess and George a note. I'm comforted knowing that at least somebody will understand our fate."

Eliza led the way up the trail, which immediately turned into a long steep flight of stairs that hugged the hill like a ladder. We climbed on and on, struggling to hold on to the steps and our flashlights at the same time. I could hear Eliza's ragged breathing above me as she forced herself skyward. At one point I almost dropped my flashlight, which would have crashed into the abyss of thick vegetation that lurked below us. The darkness underneath seemed like a bottomless pit full of unknown horrors, and truthfully, we would have been badly hurt if we'd fallen. The tangle of trees, brush, and volcanic rock that the stairway rose above would not have made for a soft landing.

"Ouch!" I cried, as Eliza stepped on my hand.

"Sorry, Nancy," she gasped. "I had to take a rest. Don't forget, this is the second time I've climbed these stairs in one evening. Are you okay?"

"I'm fine," I answered. "I'm just grateful you agreed to come here twice tonight."

"I think we're almost there," she announced.

Eliza was right. Another ten stairs and we found ourselves on a steep dirt trail that snaked through huge tropical trees and climbing vines. As we trudged along, I shone my flashlight to either side, curious to see what lay nearby. Were there animals watching us from the inky depths? Night birds? The vegetation was so thick that there was no way we could wander off the trail in the dark and get lost. At times sharp fronds slapped my face in a sneak attack, and vines creeping down from on high brushed over my skin like spider webs. Even though I don't believe in ghosts, my heart was pounding. Suddenly Eliza stopped, and I bumped against her. "Sorry, Eliza!"

"We've gone far enough, Nancy. Time to turn back."

"What?"

"I don't know why the Marchers aren't out anymore," Eliza declared, "but if they were, we would have seen them by now, for sure."

"Is this where you saw them earlier?"

"It's hard to tell in the darkness exactly where I saw them. It's not as if there are landmarks on this trail. But I think we've given them plenty of time to appear. I'm tired, Nancy. It's been a long night and I want to go home."

I shone my flashlight as close to Eliza's face as I could without annoying her. Even in the dimness, her eyes had a stubborn glow. "I don't believe Mildred was taken by the Night Marchers, Eliza," I said. "If you want to go home, okay, but you haven't proven to me that they exist."

"Nancy, that's absurd. Just because we haven't seen them doesn't mean they don't exist—you can't prove a negative," she added, raising her chin defiantly.

I shrugged. "It seems a shame to come all this way and give up so soon. I don't feel as if we've been on the trail for that long."

"Seems to me like ages," Eliza retorted. She caught sight of the determined look I shot her and dropped her gaze.

"Look, Eliza, your cousin, Mildred, is missing," I said. "If you think you've had a hard time tonight, just think about her. We've got to find her!"

Eliza sighed. "Well, if you insist, Nancy, I know of one other place where the Night Marchers might be. But we have to drive there."

"Excellent! I knew you'd come through for Mildred, Eliza. Where is this place?"

"It's not too far—about fifteen minutes away maybe. It's an ancient Hawaiian ceremonial site on a North Shore bluff. Legend has it that three British sailors were sacrificed there two centuries ago." Eliza widened her eyes dramatically and intoned, "Human sacrifices, you understand."

"I understand. But how horrible! Had the sailors attacked the Hawaiians, or were they just in the wrong place at the wrong time?"

"I don't know, Nancy. I went to visit the site only once, and I can't remember the details. Anyway, do you want to go there or not?"

"Of course I want to go, and the sooner, the better!"

I lost track of time during the hard dark slog back to the car, but once we were on the road, the distance matched Eliza's prediction perfectly. After about ten minutes she turned left onto a road that wound by the beach. Five more minutes brought us to a narrow dirt road that curved up a steep hill through jungle foliage. Then suddenly we were on the bluff. *The* bluff, as in, where the doomed British sailors had supposedly met their fates.

"Well, here we are," Eliza said as she turned off the ignition. "No Night Marchers around that I can see. We'd best be getting home, Nancy."

I jumped out of the car without bothering to answer Eliza. Ghosts or no ghosts, this place was awesome. Below us the Pacific Ocean spread a dark canvas as huge as the sky, with moonlit whitecaps flickering across it. Even though we were on a plateau above the sea, those waves looked huge. The spectacle was fantastic—creepy and beautiful all at once.

My eye caught sight of a brass plaque describing the history. I could barely read it in the moonlight, but I could see across the field to a stone foundation that marked the remnants of the ancient site.

So this was the last scene those British sailors saw. . . .

But I couldn't stay lost in my thoughts for long. Mildred was missing, and we had to find her. I flicked on my flashlight and shone it around.

"Do you think that Mildred might have come here from the airport on the way to your house?" I asked as Eliza joined me.

Eliza shrugged. "My theory is that she went to wherever she thought the Night Marchers gather. See, Mildred doesn't believe in them—she's the skeptical sort—so she wouldn't have cared that it was daytime. But she may have wanted to get a description of where the legend claims they hang out, just to give her book authenticity."

"But if the Night Marchers march along old battlegrounds, that probably includes lots of places in Hawaii," I reasoned.

"Yes, but the places I took you tonight are the places I know about. I read about them in some newspaper article on Hawaiian myths, and then I described them to Mildred over the phone shortly before she came. I was trying to do her a favor and help out her research."

"Hmm. So it *is* possible she found her way to either of these places after she arrived."

"Very possible, before she was taken by the Marchers."

I looked around the site, shining my flashlight and

casting my detective's eye over every detail. And then I saw it—something white fluttering between the stones of the old foundation.

I hurried over and grabbed it, a note written in a hasty scrawl. *Help me!* it said. *The Night Marchers are here! Mildr* The handwriting was cut off as if the writer had no more time to finish.

8

Whose Handwriting?

L et me see it!" Eliza said, grabbing the note and scanning it. She raised her eyes to mine triumphantly. "Nancy, I was right. Mildred was kidnapped by the Night Marchers. You asked for proof that they exist, and here it is!"

"But this note isn't proof!" I said as she waved it in my face. "We don't even know who wrote it."

"Are you blind, Nancy? It has Mildred's name on it."

I studied Eliza's expression. Her face yielded nothing except scorn for my comment. Then something else flickered in her eyes. Doubt about her theory? Guilt? My own eyes narrowed as I looked at her. Could she have taken Mildred, then planted the note to get me off track? Despite Eliza's fear of the Night

75

Marchers, she'd led me to this place. What if she'd been putting on an act, pretending to have spotted the Marchers earlier tonight when she'd really been planting the note?

I inspected the stones of the old foundation for more clues. Thanks to the midnight shower Eliza had spoken of earlier, the ground below them was muddy, and the mud was a deep red, like the dirt on her clothes. Maybe she'd been looking for a place to plant the note on the first trail, decided it was too remote and jungly, then came here instead. That would explain her scratches, and this place would explain the mud. One false step, and all those sharp leaves and vines on the first trail could really mess someone up.

"Hey, Eliza, can I have the note back?" I asked. "I need it for evidence." I wanted to check the handwriting against her diary, but I didn't tell Eliza that.

"Sure thing, Nancy," Eliza said, thrusting it into my hand. "I'm just so thankful we finally have a clue."

"Me too."

We climbed back into the car, and Eliza's triumphant mood quickly faded to gloom. After turning the ignition key, she bowed her head down onto the steering wheel. "Mildred must be dead," she wailed. "I'm too upset to drive home."

I gave Eliza a hug. Despite my suspicions, I had to

give her the benefit of the doubt—at least until I uncovered more evidence against her. "I'll drive if you can't," I offered. "And don't worry, Eliza. I have a feeling Mildred is alive. And I plan to find her."

Eliza appeared not to hear me. "Nancy, at first I was happy that you found the note, because it supports my belief in the Night Marchers and my theory that Mildred ran into them. But it also means I'm never going to see her again."

"Of course you'll see her. We just have to stay focused on our search."

Eliza turned her tear-streaked face to mine. "Oh, Nancy, I was right. Poor Mildred has been killed by the Night Marchers. If only she'd chosen a different subject for her mystery novel, she'd be alive now."

I took a deep breath. Okay, enough arguing for one night. As the eastern sky began to lighten, I drove us home, keeping my thoughts to myself.

Sunshine streamed in through the blinds. I opened my eyes, only to see Bess and George staring down at me. "Finally, you're awake!" George exclaimed. "How can you sleep so soundly with all this racket going on?"

George had a point. The house was alive with birdsongs, squawks, and high-pitched calls at ear-splitting decibels. Maybe the noise wouldn't have been so bad if I'd had a good night's sleep.

Speaking of which . . .

I jumped out of bed. "Is Eliza still here?" I asked. If she wasn't, the note and the diary were getting checked out, pronto.

"She's finishing breakfast," Bess said, frowning. "She seems really upset, but she won't tell us why."

I dug into my duffel bag for a pair of shorts and a T-shirt. Once dressed, I hurried into the kitchen to join Eliza. "Hi! How do you feel?" I asked.

The answer was obvious. Eliza hovered mournfully over her untouched cereal before taking a tiny bite. Then, dropping her spoon with a clatter, she darted aimlessly around the room, her hair uncombed and her blouse buttons askew. "Where are my keys?" she moaned. "I can't find them anywhere. Oh! There they are. Right on the kitchen counter." She pounced upon them like a bird on a worm. "Nancy, I'm sorry I can't talk. I'm late for work. And I can't help thinking about Mildred."

"Eliza, calm down. I told you, I'm determined to find her."

"Don't you see? It's too late for that, Nancy. You might as well go home. Anyway, I'll see you later— that is, if you decide to stay on." She rushed out the front door in a flurry of birds, jangling keys, and untucked shirttails.

The moment she left, the cacophony in the house

grew even louder. "She's gone!" shouted Jack. I tried to calm him by speaking to him gently in low tones. After a few minutes the birds finally hushed, and George, Bess, and I sat on the living-room sofa together, drinking our morning coffee.

"What's Eliza's problem today?" Bess wondered. "Yesterday she seemed so calm and organized. And perfectly dressed."

I told my friends about our adventure last night, and Bess's eyes widened.

"No such thing as ghosts, by the way, Bess!" George scoffed. "Just thought I'd remind you."

Bess shot George a withering look. "The ghosts don't spook me. The note does. I mean, if Mildred really wrote it, something terrible must have happened to her. And I know it wasn't ghosts, George, thank you very much."

I dug the note out of my sweatshirt pocket. "Here, guys, let's take a good look at it, and please let me know what you think. I could use some fresh opinions, based on logic this time."

George cracked a smile. "You mean Eliza's opinion wasn't logical?"

"She's cool!" Jack screeched, and we all started.

"Shh!" Bess scolded as the parrot glared peevishly from his cage.

We studied the note. George said, "Maybe Mildred

did write it, and she confused a gang of robbers with ghosts."

"Hope not," Bess said grimly. I agreed. We had to consider all possibilities, but that was the one I liked least. Because if Mildred had been attacked by robbers, then where was she now? How would we ever find her?

"You know, guys, someone else could have written the note," George suggested. "Her attacker may have been trying to leave a false clue."

I shrugged. "Maybe. She could have been abducted at the airport and the person planted that note to get us off track."

"Or she took a detour from the airport on her own," George said, "and she met with someone bad at the ancient site."

"How likely is it that Mildred took a detour to the site on her way from the airport?" Bess wondered. "She must have been tired from her trip, and she had to have known Eliza would be waiting for her at home."

"Sure, a detour is far-fetched," I said, "but possible, especially because Mildred is supposed to be kind of eccentric. She might have been excited about being in Hawaii after her long flight and keyed up to do research. Maybe she figured Eliza wouldn't care about waiting an extra half hour."

"Ed said she was absentminded," George declared. "So if she was hot on a project, she might not think about anything else but that."

"I can relate," I said, and grinned. Then I remembered. "Now that Eliza is gone, we can compare her handwriting to the note's."

"Do you really think Eliza could have written it?" Bess asked.

"We'll see." My friends followed me into Eliza's bedroom and watched as I took out her diary and opened to a random page. We studied her handwriting for a moment. "Totally different," I declared, and it was true: Eliza's thin, spidery writing was nothing like the large, round, bold letters of the note.

I did a double take. The handwriting in her diary entry was one thing, but how about the meaning of her words?

Went to Granddad's funeral today—so sad, she wrote. *If only Mildred and Company weren't in the picture, I'd inherit* all *his money!*

9

Sea Monster

She has a motive!" Bess cried with an excited leap. "You were *so* right to suspect her, Nancy!"

I closed the diary. Evidence was piling up against Eliza for sure, but more was needed. And I had to keep my mind alert for other suspects just in case my hunch was wrong. Still, there was no question about it: Eliza might look like an angel, but she wasn't one.

"Let's call Ed and Harriet," I announced, placing the diary back in the drawer. "I need them to fax me something." I hurried into the living room where I'd noticed a fax machine on Eliza's desk.

"Are you going to tell them about Eliza?" George asked.

"You'll see." I took my cell phone from my purse and punched in the number of Crime Time Books.

"Hi, Harriet?" I said, when her voice came on the line. "This is Nancy Drew. Could you do me a favor and fax me a sample of Mildred's handwriting if you've got one?"

"No problem, Nancy," Harriet said. "Mildred asked me to feed her cats, so I've got lengthy instructions in her typical large scrawl. I'll fax the paper to you right away." After I'd finished giving her the fax number, she asked me about the case.

"We're making progress," I answered, which was all she needed to know.

Ten minutes later the fax came through. George and Bess peered over my shoulder as we compared the handwriting in the fax with the note. "A dead ringer!" Bess cried. "Though I'm no expert on the subject, of course."

"I'm not either," I admitted, "but I totally agree with you, Bess. This note looks as if Mildred wrote it, all right."

"So what do we do now?" George asked. "Tell the police that Mildred was abducted at the historic site?"

"First I'd like to confirm with the police that the handwriting is actually Mildred's. We could be wrong." I shoved the two papers into my backpack, then thought of something else. "I also want the police to confirm that Eliza had nothing to do with writing the note. It's possible she's a really good forger. Let me grab her diary." Seconds later, I'd added the diary to the stuff in my backpack. "I think we're all set. I just hope we get back before Eliza does."

"If this case has taught me anything, it's to keep my diary tightly secured," Bess proclaimed.

"Or at least make it less embarrassing than Eliza's," George advised.

We called the police station for directions and made an appointment with Officer Kona. Once there, we submitted the diary, note, and fax before being introduced to Officer Kona, a small middle-aged woman with short dark hair and a no-nonsense manner. "It's really nice to meet you," I told her. "I'm Nancy Drew, a detective helping with the case, and these are my friends, George Fayne and Bess Marvin."

Officer Kona nodded curtly. "Ms. Bingham never mentioned that she had hired a private detective."

"Mildred's friends in San Francisco asked us to find her," I explained. "They couldn't come to Hawaii themselves because of work."

"Well, the handwriting analysis will take at least an hour," Officer Kona remarked.

"Have you found out anything else about the case?" I asked.

"No, I'm afraid we haven't," she said. "And I'm not sure office protocol allows me to share confidential information with you anyway, young lady. So why don't you have a seat in the waiting room or call back later for the results of the handwriting analysis?"

I exchanged frustrated looks with my friends. Despite Officer Kona's efficient manner, I had a strong suspicion she wasn't throwing herself into solving the case. She was treating it like a day job when a missing person was at stake!

I sighed. What could we do while we waited? I had to do *something*. Hanging out here was not an option. I mean, right now Mildred could be stuck somewhere, imprisoned, and we were her only hope for rescue. So far Eliza was our only suspect. It was time to branch out and consider others.

The question was, who?

My mind clicked away as I reviewed all the info on Mildred I'd learned so far, like who had officially seen her last. I turned to my friends. "Do you guys remember the name of the person Mildred sat next to on the plane to Honolulu? Wasn't it somebody with a last name like Ching? Jamey, I think."

George snapped her fingers. "Yeah, that's it."

I smiled. "Jamey Ching," I repeated thoughtfully. "Sure, he said Mildred had disappeared into the crowd of passengers at the airport when they arrived.

But what if he wasn't telling the whole story? He might know more than he's admitting."

"We could probably ask the police for his number," George suggested. "They've already been in touch with him."

I shot a look at Officer Kona while she worked on some papers at her desk to our right. Would she give me Jamey's number?

Only one way to find out.

"I've spoken with Jamey myself," she told us after I asked for his number. With an impatient wave, she added, "I assure you, he knows nothing. He had to rush to make his connecting flight to Maui, so he barely noticed Mildred once they'd disembarked. He told us she was swallowed up by the throng of passengers. He's not going to be able to add anything else."

"Still, I'd like to talk to him," I pressed.

"I told you, we've already done that. We questioned him thoroughly, and he checks out. He's not the type to abduct old ladies."

"What type is he?" I asked, curious.

"A surfer," Officer Kona replied. "Your typical laid-back surfer dude. The only difference between Jamey Ching and many other surfers is that he actually has a job teaching it. He works at a Maui hotel instructing tourists. We've spoken to his boss and learned that he's very dependable, harmless, and uninvolved. What more can I say?"

Dependable. Harmless. Uninvolved. I'd heard those claims before. I wanted to judge for myself whether they were true.

"Anyway, I'm afraid I can't give you his number," she added sourly. "It's not our policy to reveal confidential information to strangers."

"Even if I'm a detective who could help you solve the case?"

"That's correct."

I sighed. On to the next plan. Obviously the police weren't rolling out any red carpets for us. I would have to find Jamey's number myself. But that was fine with me when directory assistance was just a phone call away. I knew Jamey's last name, and that he lived on Maui. As long as he was listed in directory assistance, we'd be okay.

"Come on, guys," I said to Bess and George, "let's go for a walk while we wait." I thanked Officer Kona politely. After all, we needed her cooperation with the handwriting analysis. Smiling tightly, she suggested we call her in an hour for the report.

Once outside, I whipped out my cell phone and called Maui directory assistance, asking for Jamey Ching's phone number. I got the listing for a James Ching. I punched in the call.

The phone rang and rang until a machine picked up. A male voice claiming to be Jamey Ching advised daytime callers to call him at the Blue Wave Hotel. He provided the number before signing off.

I punched it in. "Surf Shack. Jamey Ching speaking!" barked a youthful voice once the hotel receptionist put me through.

"Uh, hi, my name is Nancy Drew," I said, surprised at my luck in reaching him on this sunny morning.

"Excuse me, I'm eating an early lunch," he said as faint munching sounds echoed across the wire. "Have to fuel up before my lessons this afternoon. How can I help you, Nancy?"

"I'm a private detective investigating the disappearance of an older woman," I told him. "I believe you sat next to her on the plane."

"Oh, Mildred! Right," he said. "A real cool lady. Adventurous for someone her age. Anyway, I told the police everything I know, which isn't much. So I dunno how much help I can be."

"Would you mind going over again whatever you remember?" I asked. "The smallest details can be important. Maybe the police didn't pick up on something."

"Okay, let me think. Well, I sat next to Mildred on the plane, and when she got off, she just blended into the crowd."

"Did you guys talk about anything particular?"

"Just that she was looking forward to visiting her cousin in Honolulu. I take it she was planning to crash with her," he added.

"So you didn't see Mildred again after she disappeared into the crowd at the terminal?" I asked.

"Nope. But I can't believe she's just *poof,* vanished. That is too weird!"

"Did you notice anything else unusual about Mildred during the flight? Maybe something she did?"

"No, Nancy, sorry," Jamey said. "As I said, wish I could help ya."

"Well, thanks for talking to me, Jamey."

"Anytime." After we hung up, I was silent for a moment, lost in thought.

"So?" George said. Bess tilted her head curiously.

I described our conversation. "Jamey sounds convincing, guys, but you know me. I like to meet people before I judge them."

"Uh-oh," Bess moaned. "I know what's coming next."

"A trip to Maui?" George asked happily.

"Why not?" I said. "The Hawaiian islands aren't far from one another. A trip to Maui might not take all that long. Let's at least find out."

I ducked back into the police station, where the receptionist gave me the names of some in-state airlines. Once outside again, I reserved a flight to Maui and a room at the Blue Wave Hotel from my cell phone.

George shot me a wry smile. "It's lucky your detective instincts are time-tested, Nancy. Chasing down a surfer dude on Maui seems like a total wild card, if you ask me."

Bess frowned. "I don't know, George. I think we're stuck in a rut here in Honolulu. We haven't had much progress in the case, and there's nothing so suspicious about Eliza to keep us from other leads."

"That is so wrong!" George cried. "I mean, if Eliza isn't suspicious, then who is? Think about the clues we've found pointing to her: the diary, the dress, her grandfather's inheritance. The list goes on."

"No, it doesn't," Bess said firmly. "It stops right there. That's the problem. We're stuck."

"What about the note, then?" George pointed out. "When you think about it, that's another clue. And you know why? Because I bet Eliza led you to it on purpose, Nancy."

"Speaking of the note." I checked my watch. We'd been at the police station for almost an hour. Maybe the handwriting analysis was ready. "Let me check with Officer Kona about it." I popped back inside.

Officer Kona looked up at me from her desk. "Oh, are you still here, Nancy? You're in luck, because the handwriting expert just handed me his report. Neither of the samples you gave us matches the note. Someone else wrote it and tried to make the writing look like Mildred's."

Relief! So Mildred hadn't met some horrible fate at the historic site. Or at least that possibility seemed a lot less likely now.

"Are you sure that the writer of the diary couldn't have forged the note?"

Officer Kona shrugged. "Our expert says no. That's all I can tell you."

"Okay, well thanks very much, Officer Kona. This information is really helpful."

"I don't know how," she said. "Because it doesn't tell us who wrote the note. But we'll keep on plugging away at the case, don't you worry."

I did worry, though. Because Mildred was still missing, and the police weren't making things easy for me. Once outside, I told my friends the news: that according to the handwriting expert, neither Mildred nor Eliza had written the note.

"What a relief that Mildred didn't write it!" Bess exclaimed. "That means she wasn't at the site."

"Although I guess she could have been there, and someone other than Eliza forged the note," I said.

"Far-fetched," George said, and honestly, I agreed.

"Now let's hurry to Eliza's house. We need to put

back her diary, pack, and call a cab. I don't want to miss the next flight out. But first," I added, cell phone in hand, "let me call Eliza at work to let her know we won't be staying at her house tonight. I'll give her the number of the Blue Wave Hotel in case she needs to reach us."

I thought about the note on our short flight to Maui, but I was no closer to figuring it out. Officer Kona was right. Maybe we knew who didn't write the note, but we were still a long way from knowing who did. I vowed to check out a sample of Jamey's handwriting as soon as we could scare one up.

We checked into the Blue Wave Hotel, a luxurious place on a sunny Maui beach packed with tanned tourists. Despite a smattering of fancy hotels, Maui seemed a lot less developed than Oahu. Only minutes after we left the airport in our rental car bound for the Blue Wave, we were surrounded by lush green sugar-cane fields. A gigantic volcano named Haleakala loomed ten thousand feet above us. Though its summit was hidden in a puffy white cloud, sunlight poured down on emerald green pineapple fields that carpeted its slopes. In the distance, the dazzling blue-green sea shone brightly.

After changing into our bathing suits, we hit the beach. I wanted to find Jamey ASAP because the afternoon sun was already sliding toward the sea. Who knew how much longer he'd be giving surfing lessons today?

The sand was hot, and our flip-flops kicked it onto the backs of our legs as we hunted for the perfect spot to read and hang out. Bess and I wore bikinis; George wore surf shorts and a bikini top. Soon we found an unoccupied beach umbrella and set up shop.

A waiter came by with a tray of drinks just as we were spreading our towels on the sand. "Could I interest you girls in some ice-cold coconut-pineapple juice?" he asked.

"Sure, thanks," George said, and we all took glasses. Soon we'd settled on our towels, sipping drinks and gazing out to sea. "This sure is the life," she added.

"If we could only get a lead on Mildred," I said. "I can't enjoy anything till we've found her." I stood up and put my empty glass on the roaming waiter's tray. "Come on, guys, let's find Jamey's Surf Shack. We've got some lessons to take."

"Count me out," Bess said, adjusting her dark glasses. "I'll hold down the fort here with my drink and my book." She lifted her glass happily in a toast.

"Are you sure, Bess? Those waves look fantastic," George said, scanning the perfectly formed waves that were neither too big nor too small.

"So does the beach," Bess said, stretching her

legs like a cat. "I'll go for a swim later, once I've warmed up."

"Okay," George said, "have fun."

George and I investigated a lean-to we'd noticed on the other side of the hotel's beach entrance. Sure enough, a sign on it said SURF SHACK! in large, colorful, zigzaggy letters. A painted, vertical surfboard hovering over a dot served as the exclamation point. Inside the open window of the shack, a young man with shoulder-length dark hair, a golden tan, and broad shoulders was busy writing notes. I guessed he was around our age.

Before we came any closer, I stopped George and whispered, "George, I don't want him to know I'm the girl who called him with questions about Mildred. He'll realize I'm a detective. I've got to think of an alias."

"Any ideas?" George asked.

I shrugged. "Something simple and easy to remember, like Nancy Marvin!"

"Then Bess can be Bess Drew," George said with a chuckle. "If they meet, that is."

I led the way to the shack's window and greeted Jamey. He looked up, blinking, his hazel eyes slowly focusing on us.

"Huh? Oh, hi," he sputtered, shooting us a lopsided grin. "Sorry, I was writing in my log." He held up a spiral notebook as if to prove his point. "Anyway, how can I help you gals?"

"We want to take surfing lessons," George said. "The hotel receptionist told us to ask for Jamey Ching at the Surf Shack."

"That's me! Jamey at your service." His handsome face clouded over as he glanced at his watch. "Whoops! It's almost four o'clock. A bit late for lessons. See, I usually like to close up shop—or shack, *heh!*—by then."

"Usually?" I asked, smiling coyly. "You mean you're not always so strict?"

"Oh, I'm not strict, ladies. Not strict at all." He shot us another grin, then set down his logbook and peered out to sea. "Awesome conditions. Too good to pass up, man. The waves were rougher earlier in the day, so you gals chose the right time. Have you ever surfed before?"

"We're not beginners," I said, "but it has been a while."

"Cool! Then let's get started. As you know, my name is Jamey. Yours?"

Without missing a beat, George said, "She's Nancy Marvin, and I'm George Fayne. Nice to meet you, Jamey!"

Five minutes later Jamey was leading us across the sand to the water, holding his surfboard casually under his arm. Our surfboards, which he'd chosen for us, were kind of heavy, and I held on to mine with both hands. Soon we were in the water, flat on our boards, paddling out to sea. Jamey coached us on a few things.

"Don't get too close to each other," he shouted. "Stay at least thirty feet apart so we won't crash."

Then, finally, the moment of truth. "This is it, girls!" he bellowed as a wave swelled up. "She's as good as they get!" Hopping onto his board, Jamey began to surf down the wave, and George and I were happy to take his cue. Leaping onto my feet, I crouched on my board, arms out, while bracing my legs apart for balance. As I zoomed down the crest of the wave, my legs wobbled at first, but quickly grew steadier. The sea water gently sprayed my face, making tiny prisms as the sun glistened on the drops around me. Remembering Jamey's tips, I maneuvered the board along the wave just ahead of the breaking point.

But the good feeling didn't last long. The wave tossed me off the board as the crest caught up to me.

Like a monster from the depths, the wave grabbed me, pulling me down inside it, rolling me around as if it were swallowing me for lunch. With burning lungs, I shot to the surface again, no harm done.

Then I saw the fin.

10

Cluing In

Shark!" **I screamed, glancing** wildly around for George and Jamey. Out of the corner of my eye, I saw them about fifty feet away, catching another wave. I was closer to shore than they were, but the shark was closer to me. As if it sensed my thoughts, the shark's fin turned toward me like a deadly periscope. Then it shot my way.

"Shark!" I screamed again. Over another breaking wave I saw Jamey's head swivel toward me. A split second was all it took for him to clue in to my predicament. With his arms flailing, he gestured to George to get to shore. The lifeguard noticed too.

The lifeguard lifted a bullhorn from a hook on the side of his chair. "Everyone, out of the water! Shark!" he bellowed.

It was as if an electric shock had jolted through the peaceful community of sunbathers and swimmers. Parents rushed to the water, calling in their kids, while panicky swimmers shot toward the beach, riding every wave they could to safety. Meanwhile Jamey was already heading my way, his arms making swift cuts through the water and his legs kicking up a geyser of foam. But what good could he do against a shark? Especially when it was between us, and headed for the kill?

I had to save myself. I rolled onto my surfboard and lay flat, my chest heaving for air against the fiberglass surface. Then I propped myself on my elbows to face the shark.

A second later it gushed up before me with all its flashing teeth. The shark's mouth was like an upside-down V filled with more razor blades than you can count, a sight to see in nightmares for the rest of my life. If I was lucky enough to have one . . .

Within a few seconds, like a person leafing through a phone book hunting for a name, my mind shuffled through tons of shark-escape ideas before rejecting them. And then I remembered something I'd read in a book. Something about punching sharks in the nose if they attack you.

I barely had time. This had to work.

I clenched my right fist, drew it back, and *wham!* I

punched that shark in the nose harder than I've ever punched anything in my life, even the toughest criminal.

The shark hesitated, his nose in the air. This wasn't the time for a job half done. Drawing my fist back again, I punched the shark again, even harder. Pain radiated through my hand, and my whole arm shook with the impact. I just hoped I hadn't scratched my hand. Blood in a shark's nose would *not* be good.

The shark froze. Then, like some sort of awful robot, it swirled around and swam away.

I had to get to shore! I looked over my shoulder. Where was the perfect wave when I needed it? I wasn't waiting around for perfection, though. A small wave, too wimpy to make for a great ride in, came along, and I was on my board riding it without a second thought.

It got me far enough. A few moments later I was on the beach, surrounded by Jamey, George, Bess, the lifeguard, and various other sunbathers and swimmers.

"Are you okay, Nancy?" Jamey asked, his eyes scanning me to make sure. "You were awesome with that shark."

"I'm fine, thanks," I replied, flashing Jamey a grateful smile. Even though he hadn't actually helped me, there was no doubt in my mind that he was a genuine sweetheart. His concern seemed sincere. The idea that he could have hurt Mildred suddenly seemed bizarre. I mean, what was I thinking?

"Nancy, you were something out there," Bess said, smiling with relief.

"You showed that shark who's boss!" George added. "I could practically see its tail tucking under as it swam away in disgrace."

"I'm gonna punch a shark in the nose if I ever meet one, just like you did," a small boy told me.

"Well, I hope you won't ever meet one. It's a pretty rare thing, even if you spend lots of time swimming in the ocean," I said, trying to reassure him.

"You were just unlucky," he declared.

I smiled. "Guess so. But look on the bright side. Maybe I used up all my bad luck by meeting that shark, so now my good luck will begin."

"Your luck began when that shark swam away," George pointed out. "Let's hope you're on a roll now, Nancy."

I gave her the thumbs-up sign. "Hope so."

I glanced at Jamey, whose attention had wandered to Bess. "Are you with Nancy and George?" he asked her, smiling. What is it about my friend that makes an instant impression on all the guys she meets?

"Sure am. I'm Bess Marvin," she told him, smiling back.

"Oh! Nancy's sister?"

Uh-oh.

Bess shot me a puzzled look before a flash of understanding crossed her face. No doubt about it, Bess was fast. "Nancy's my cousin," she answered brightly.

"Gotcha," Jamey said, appraising the two of us. "Makes sense. I mean, you gals look sort of alike. Similar hair color and all." Studying George, he added, "So you're just a friend of the family, huh? Along for the ride? I mean, you've gotta admit you look nothing like Bess or Nancy."

"Nope. I guess you could say we're not at all alike," George said, trading a grin with Bess.

"How would you like to celebrate my luck this afternoon by having dinner with us?" I asked Jamey.

"Uh . . . sure!" he said, with an eager glance at Bess. Then, frowning, he added, "I just remembered—I'm supposed to have dinner with my sister, Robin."

"Then bring her too," George suggested. "The more the merrier!"

"Okay," Jamey said. "There's a Polynesian restaurant called the Four Winds in this awesome little fishing village near the hotel. Want to meet there around seven?"

"Sure," I said. "See you then."

As we waited for our dinners to arrive at the Four Winds, Bess asked Jamey how he liked it in Hawaii.

"I love my job," he said as a waiter brought us pineapple-juice smoothies. "I don't get how surfers can be happy on the Mainland during the winter months. Here it's warm all the time. Maybe I'll go to college in Hawaii someday, but right now I'm cool with the way things are—my job and all."

"What about you, Robin?" Bess asked, turning to Jamey's sister. "How do you like living on Maui?"

Robin shrugged. She was about six or seven years older than Jamey and shared his shoulder-length dark hair and tan skin, but her build was slight and delicate. "I'm not as crazy about life in paradise as Jamey is. See, I want to be a college professor. Living in a college town or an exciting city on the Mainland would suit me just fine."

"So are you in college now?" I asked as the waiter served our dinners.

"I'm postgraduate, actually," she said. "I'm getting my PhD in Hawaiian mythology."

"Really?" I replied, perking up. "Are you studying any particular myths?"

Robin nodded. "My main interest is the volcano goddess, Pele. I'm writing my dissertation on her."

Bess, George, and I shared a look. Hawaiian mythology—what a perfect introduction to the subject of Mildred! "That's so weird, Robin," I began, "because a woman we know of named Mildred—she's a friend

102

of some friends—had been writing about Hawaiian mythology when she disappeared. But not about Pele. She'd been researching the legend of the Night Marchers for a mystery book. Have either of you heard anything about her? She disappeared in Honolulu. I'm sure there would have been media coverage."

Robin and Jamey shifted in their seats, and averted their eyes. After a moment, Jamey blurted out, "Actually, I sat next to Mildred on the plane from San Francisco to Honolulu."

"Really?" I said, trying my best to look surprised. "What were you doing in San Francisco?"

Jamey glanced at Robin, then back at me. "Robin's professor—his name is Alex Kahilua—was interviewing for teaching jobs around San Francisco. He invited me to go with him to look at colleges there." He shrugged. "I've kinda been checking out colleges. I mean, Robin wants me to go, and so do our parents, but I'd miss Hawaii too much. If I go to college, it won't be on the Mainland."

"Why didn't you fly straight back to Maui, then?" George asked. "Don't they have direct flights here?"

"The flights to Maui were booked," Jamey explained, "and Alex needed to be in Honolulu anyway to teach a class. So I hopped a flight to Maui alone once we landed."

"And Mildred just disappeared?" I asked.

Once again, Jamey shifted in his seat. "Yeah, she just disappeared into the crowd at the airport, like I said before."

Everyone was silent as we ate dessert. I had time to savor an awesome coconut meringue pie, and also to think about what Jamey had told me. When the waiter brought the check, Jamey took it from him quickly. "Let me take you girls out," he offered with a shy glance at Bess. "I feel responsible for your close encounter with the shark, Nancy."

"That wasn't your fault," I said. "How could you control a shark?"

"Still, this is my treat," he replied.

He whipped a pen from his pocket and began to sign the credit card receipt. "Jamey," Bess said, pointing at the pen, "is that Mildred's pen?"

Sure enough, the words *Mildred's Pen* appeared in prominent gold script along the side of the glossy black pen.

11

Surprised!

Jamey stared at the pen, looking flabbergasted. "What? Oh—I guess I must have picked it up by mistake somehow." He paused for a moment before adding, "Oh, I know how this happened! The state of Hawaii makes people coming over from the Mainland fill out a form describing any plants or animals they've got with them. Maybe Mildred and I got our pens mixed up."

I studied Jamey's handsome face. Bess was looking at it too. And from the look in her eyes, I could tell we'd come to the same conclusion. Not only was Jamey cute, but he also seemed totally sincere.

"What else do you remember about the flight, or about Mildred?" I asked.

He shrugged. "Not much. Just that we talked

about her book on the Night Marchers. She said she was real excited about coming to Hawaii and researching the legend. She mentioned staying with her cousin in Honolulu—she was heading there directly from the airport. That's it. The rest of the time we spent sleeping. Or at least I did."

I turned to Robin. "Well, you're an expert on Hawaiian legends. What do you know about the Night Marchers? Could Mildred have endangered herself while she was looking for them?"

She smiled tightly. "People who believe in the Night Marchers say they're very dangerous. Whether or not you believe in them, though, you could get hurt just by tromping around looking for them."

"Do you think there could be a real explanation for them, like a gang of robbers?" I asked. "A gang that acts like a group of ghosts, maybe to scare off the police?"

"I doubt it," Robin said. "I don't believe in ghosts, Nancy, but I also don't think the Night Marchers are supposed to look like real people. At least, I've never heard those rumors. Mildred should have been safe doing her research, unless she fell off a cliff in the dark. And it was daytime when she first went missing, right?"

"Right," I said absently. Something Jamey had said was nagging at my mind. Something about the plane flight. "What was the name of your professor, Robin? Alex something?"

"Alex Kahilua."

I turned to Jamey. "You mentioned that he didn't come back to Maui with you. Why not?"

"See, Alex lives on Maui, but he teaches a class twice a week in Honolulu," Jamey said. "Since he had to teach later that day, he decided it would be a waste of time to return to Maui for just a few hours."

"Could he have seen what happened to Mildred?" I asked.

Jamey shrugged. "I don't remember him and Mildred talking," Jamey explained in a baffled tone. "Alex might not even know who she is. But I'm sure the police questioned him because they told me they talked to all the folks who sat near Mildred. They didn't single me out, I hope. If Alex saw anything strange happening to Mildred, he would have told the police when they got in touch with him."

"Where did Alex sit?" George asked. "Was he anywhere near Mildred?"

"Alex and I made our reservations at the last minute, so we couldn't sit together. He was in the seat in front of me." Jamey yawned, covering his mouth with his hand. Were my questions getting to him? Maybe. But I had to keep going—I was hoping to discover an overlooked lead.

His sister had other ideas, though. "Jamey is obviously exhausted, and I need to get home too," Robin said, checking her watch. "But if you have more questions about Mildred, why don't you ask Alex yourself? As Jamey said, he lives right here on Maui."

I was about to ask Robin for Alex's phone number when she announced, "Wait, there he is!" Slinging her purse over her shoulder, she wove her way through the tables to the front of the restaurant, where a dark-haired man in his thirties stood at the take-out counter.

"That *is* him! Awesome coincidence," Jamey exclaimed. The four of us followed Robin's path to the take-out counter where Robin introduced me and my friends to Alex.

He was pretty much your classic introvert. With his stooped shoulders and tortoiseshell glasses, he greeted us awkwardly as Robin told him our names. "Hello, everyone," he mumbled, tucking his chin down and barely making eye contact. "It's so very nice to meet you. How are you enjoying your stay on Maui?"

"Very much, thanks," I replied. "How do you like living in a tropical paradise?"

"It's delightful," he said politely.

"Um, I hope you don't mind me asking you this question when you're just about to order your dinner," I began, "but did you notice an elderly lady on your recent flight from San Francisco to Maui? Her name is Mildred."

"No, I'm afraid I don't remember seeing anyone like that."

"Really? Oh, well. We're trying to find her," I explained. "She's missing."

"Missing!" His jaw dropped, making him look even gawkier.

"Yes, it's a long story," I said. "Didn't the police contact you for information?" When he shook his head, I added, "Anyway, thanks for answering my questions."

"I'm happy to answer them anytime," he said, sounding like a robot.

We all said good night before going our separate ways. Once in our room at the Blue Wave Hotel, my friends and I chatted about the case.

"I bet Jamey is hiding something," George said. "His answers to our questions were kind of vague. Like his explanation of that pen, for example."

"Why don't you believe that he and Mildred got their pens mixed up like he said?" Bess asked.

"I guess that explanation isn't *so* far-fetched," George said. "Still, I'm not convinced he's innocent."

"But what would his motive be?" Bess asked.

George shrugged. "There are lots of things we

don't know about this case," she added darkly.

"And not nearly enough that we *do* know," I declared.

The next day dawned sunny and hot, with a gentle breeze that rustled the pink and purple flowers twined around the railing of our balcony. The view of the ocean, with the waves breaking gently on the shore, was breathtaking.

I had no time for sightseeing, though. Mildred was still missing! Time to really buckle down.

I didn't think Jamey could possibly be guilty, but I wanted to confirm my hunch with evidence. If I was careful, maybe I could snatch a copy of his handwriting. What about that logbook he'd been so busy writing in yesterday? Sneaking a copy of that shouldn't be a problem. Halfway through our breakfast of pineapple pancakes, I told my friends my thoughts, then left them eating in the hotel dining room while I went outside to do some research.

As I walked along the beach, all sorts of questions were churning in my mind. But the main ones were these: Who took Mildred? Where is she now? And who wrote the note?

I approached the Surf Shack and saw Jamey inside, his dark head bent down over his logbook. Was his job all paperwork and no lessons? Frustrated, I strolled far enough away so he wouldn't notice me. Time to restrategize.

While I stood in the shade of a palm tree thinking, my mind switched back to Eliza. What about that inheritance she'd mentioned in her diary—the one supposedly left by her grandfather to Mildred? And who was the "Company" she'd mentioned when she'd wished that Mildred and Company weren't in the picture? I hadn't had time to follow up on that clue yet, but why not pursue it now?

I glanced around the beach to make sure no one could hear me—not that it would be a big deal if someone could. I mean, Eliza was a whole island away. But careful detective habits are tough to break.

No one was near, so I took my cell phone from my shorts pocket and punched in Ed and Harriet's work number. Since they knew Mildred well, they might know her grandfather's last name and how to get a copy of his will. If he'd left all his money to Mildred, as Eliza had claimed, would the inheritance go to Eliza if Mildred was gone? Because if those were the terms of the will, Eliza would definitely have a motive. A giant one.

"Crime Time Books," a receptionist said on the second ring.

"Hi, this is Nancy Drew. Could I speak to Ed or Harriet?"

"No, I'm sorry. Neither one is here. Could I take a message?"

I left my name and cell phone number, then returned to Bess and George. I found them as they were leaving the dining room. "Any luck with Jamey?" George asked.

I shook my head. "He's still in the shack. I'll have to wait till he leaves."

"Listen, Nancy," Bess said, "if you and George want to do other things, I'd be happy to sneak a copy of Jamey's handwriting as soon as he's gone. All I have to do is sit on the beach and watch him from far enough away so he won't notice me. I think I can handle the job," she added, flashing a sly smile. "If it turns out he's guilty, I'll have helped our cause."

George hooted. "You're so selfless, Bess—you're always taking the tough jobs."

"It's all a matter of patience, George," Bess said playfully. "Luckily that's one of my main virtues. I must admit, though, that being surrounded by cute boys on a Hawaiian beach will be a big test of it—so wish me luck."

I laughed, but as I listened to my friend's jokes, the truth was that I felt torn. Oahu beckoned, and I was in a hurry to get back there. Was it worth waiting around on Maui just to write off an unlikely suspect? The forged note was such a big clue, the biggest one we'd found so far; it hinted that Oahu was probably the place for us to be.

I told Bess and George my thoughts.

George shook her head sadly. "No one would listen when I warned that Eliza was guilty. But Nancy, don't you think since we're here, we might as well finish our job? With a copy of Jamey's writing, we can officially cross him off our list. That'll make us feel better."

I bit my lip, hesitating. I guess George made sense, up to a point. "Well, if it doesn't take too long, okay," I said. "We've come this far. What's another hour or so? I mean, Jamey teaches surfing, doesn't he? He'll have to leave his shack sometime."

"And you know what?" Bess added. "There's always a tiny chance he *is* guilty. Even if he is nice." She squinted her eyes and scanned our sun-splashed surroundings. "Hey, why don't you guys take an hour and do something fun while I get to work? Nancy, I bet you could use some downtime to clear your mind for when we return to Eliza. You've been worrying about Mildred nonstop."

I smiled. "Well, that's how I solve cases—by being constantly focused. But I think you're right, Bess. Taking an hour to clear my mind is a great idea. It'll help me gain a fresh perspective on what we've learned."

George said, "My guidebook described this great place on Maui called the Iao Valley. It's a nature preserve, and it's supposed to be one of the wettest places on earth. Apparently, the sun can be out at the beach without a cloud in sight, and it'll be raining in the Iao Valley."

"Woohoo! A break from the heat," I said. "Let's get going, George. And Bess, good luck!"

Our hotel concierge provided excellent directions, and I was happy to learn that the Iao Valley was only about twenty minutes away. Once there, George and I climbed out of our car in search of hiking trails. No question about it, George was right about the rain. Our sun hats instantly became rain hats, protecting us from a light misty drizzle as we strolled along paved nature paths. Bright green mountains shot skyward on each side of us, vanishing into a rain cloud that covered the valley like a thick gray blanket. Waterfalls plunged down the perpendicular slopes into a jungle of green. Behind us, where the sky was lighter, a rainbow shimmered.

"Look, George, there's a waterfall right there," I said, pointing to a spot just off the paved trail, "with room to stand under it—like in all those tourist pictures of Hawaii." We scrambled down a muddy bank and followed a dirt trail that snaked by a swiftly moving stream. In a minute we'd reached the waterfall, which was flanked by ominous signs that read CAUTION: FLASH FLOODS. The rain, which had been nothing but a floating mist, suddenly grew heavy, pouring down like a summer thunderstorm in River Heights. A crashing sound reverberated down the mountain.

A flash flood?

"Now may not be the best time to check out that waterfall," George said doubtfully. I felt a prickle of fear—my friend was usually so adventurous. The roaring grew louder. I could tell it wasn't the normal sound of the falls.

"We'd better get back to the trail!" I urged. With our sneakers slipping in the mud, we fought our way back up the bank. The moment our feet hit the pavement, I instantly relaxed.

Well, until I saw Ed and Harriet smiling at us.

12

Listening In

No need to worry, girls," Harriet told us. "It's just thunder. A lightning bolt just struck the top of that mountain behind you."

George and I exchanged looks. Worries about a flood suddenly seemed like ancient history. What I wanted to know now was what these two were doing in Hawaii! George put my thoughts into words by asking Ed and Harriet exactly that question.

"We became so worried about poor Mildred, we couldn't stand waiting any longer," Harriet said, answering George. "We hated feeling helpless."

"We called Eliza yesterday to track you girls down," Ed explained. "She said you'd come to Maui, so we popped over here from San Francisco on a direct flight to see if we could help. At the hotel, we ran into Bess, who told us where you were. She didn't want to at first, but we insisted. I'm not sure she entirely trusts us."

Once more George and I traded looks. Bess must have freaked when she saw this *extremely* resourceful couple. Guardedly, I said, "I wish I could tell you we've found Mildred, but we haven't. We're on Maui to investigate the guy she sat next to on the plane."

Harriet's face fell as I broke the news. "Well, I guess I shouldn't be surprised that you girls haven't found her," she said. "I know you would have told us. But we were hoping you'd had a bit of luck since we left home."

No wonder Ed and Harriet hadn't answered the phone today when I'd called them with my question about Eliza's grandfather and her inheritance—they were on their way here.

"So you were able to get off work to come to Maui?" I asked. "I thought you had an emergency that meant you couldn't come."

"We took care of that the day you girls flew out," Harriet said. "We were pleasantly surprised by how quickly we resolved our problem. Now, if only we could solve the Mildred problem as handily."

"We're disappointed that you haven't found Mildred, of course, Nancy," Ed said, "but I'm glad we're able to help. We drove to the Iao Valley from the hotel to get your report on the case."

"Well, dear," Harriet said, forcing a smile, "let's get back to the hotel now. I'm hungry and tired."

That was odd. They didn't want to start searching immediately? "George," I said, "we should get back too."

Once at the hotel, George and I quickly ate sandwiches at a café downstairs before returning to our room. We were greeted by Bess, who was waving a piece of paper at us excitedly from her bed. "Got it, guys! A sample of Jamey's writing. Fortunately, there's a copy machine in the Surf Shack. So I snuck in and copied a page from his logbook, which I just faxed to Officer Kona." George's portable fax machine, attached to the phone between the beds, was finishing up printing a receipt.

"Good job, Bess," I said, sitting down across from her. "So, I hear you ran into Ed and Harriet."

Bess bit her lip, and her face flushed red with guilt. "I feel so bad, Nancy. I told them where you were. But they were pestering me, and I figured they couldn't do much harm to you in broad daylight in a place with other tourists."

I laughed. "Don't worry about it, Bess. George and I can take on Ed and Harriet. But it *is* weird that they just popped up here out of the blue."

"Just when I thought we'd escaped them," Bess said.

"It's just like what happened in San Francisco," George said, "with them popping up all over the place. They have a habit of doing that, and it's pretty disturbing, if you ask me."

"So what do you think Ed and Harriet are up to, Nancy?" Bess asked.

"Who knows?" I replied, baffled. "I can't tell whether they're sincere when they claim they came here because of Mildred. I mean, if they wanted us to go so much that they bought us plane tickets, I don't see why they'd follow us."

"What's your hunch, though?" George pressed.

"I'm not saying this is likely, but here's a wild thought: What if Ed and Harriet arranged for Mildred's disappearance, and then they came to Hawaii to make it seem as if they cared about her? You know, to cover up their motive."

"I wouldn't put anything past them," Bess said darkly, "even though I'm not sure why they'd do it."

"I'm going to follow them," I said, shooting up from the bed. "I need to figure out whether they're just harmless eccentrics or dangerous criminals."

"Be careful," Bess warned.

I told her I would. As I headed for the door, the phone rang. Bess answered it. "It's not?" she said after a pause. "Okay, well, thank you so much." In less than thirty seconds, the phone call was over.

"Who was that?" George asked curiously.

"The Honolulu police getting back to me about Jamey's handwriting sample. The expert claims his writing isn't even close to the note. No way could he have written it, or even forged it."

"So now that Jamey is off the hook," George said, "shouldn't we be getting back to Honolulu where the note was found, and where Mildred was last seen?"

"Yeah, but what about Ed and Harriet?" I said. "They've thrown a new curve into our plans. Honolulu can wait until I've checked those guys out. Maybe I can find out their room number and—you know, perch close by. Listen in."

Once more I headed for the door—and this time, no phone call stopped me.

But the desk clerk downstairs did.

"My friends Ed and Harriet are staying at this hotel," I told him. "We're supposed to meet in their room and then go out for lunch. Can you please give me their room number? I'm late."

"Sorry, miss," the desk clerk said. "It's against our regulations to give out information on our guests, including room numbers. But I could call them and ask them to come down to meet you. Or I could connect you by phone and you could ask them yourself."

"No, that's okay," I said, trying not to sound frustrated. "Lunch is . . . um . . . a birthday surprise for her." I bit my lip. How to get Ed and Harriet's room number?

That's when I saw them, strolling toward a lobby elevator. My eyes focused like a telescope as I watched them disappear inside the elevator, but I kept my distance until the doors slid closed.

Then I made my move.

Hurrying over to the bank of elevators, I inspected the numbers flashing above the doors they'd entered. Their elevator was stopping on three.

I bounded up the nearby stairwell. Once on three, I cracked open the door and peeked into the corridor, only to see a door down the hallway clicking closed. I sprang over to it.

Room 315.

I looked around. Not a soul in sight. I put my ear to the door, then jerked back in surprise. The cordial Ed and Harriet were arguing really loudly.

13

The House of the Sun

Sure, my friends and I thought they were weird—but Ed and Harriet had always seemed so patient with each other. I'd never sensed there was any fighting between them. I put my ear back against the door.

"Stop crying, Harriet!" Ed yelled.

"I can't help it!" she shouted, her voice choked with loud hysterical sobs.

"Well, you'll have to!" Ed said. "I can't take it anymore."

"I can't stand the suspense," she retorted, her voice rising.

"Darling, please calm down," Ed said in a softer tone. "This isn't like you. You've worked yourself into a state. Anyway, I have every confidence in Nancy."

At the sound of my name, I pressed my ear harder to the door, not wanting to miss a syllable.

"We never should have come to Hawaii," Ed went on. "We'll just get in the way of Nancy's investigation. After all, dear, she only arrived in Hawaii two mornings ago. Give her a chance!"

"Nancy is doing a fine job," Harriet said. "But with something as terrible as Mildred disappearing, more effort can't hurt. And that means us pitching in."

"Meanwhile we're neglecting our business."

"Which is more important, Ed, our business, or the life of a missing friend?" Harriet broke into fresh sobs. "I just can't imagine what's happened to her."

I straightened up. Not only was my hearing at risk, but my ear was growing numb from pressing it to the door. Anyway, I'd heard enough. I stared at the door, dumbfounded, as the sounds of Ed and Harriet's discussion floated around me.

It seemed evidence enough that they were on the straight and narrow—they really were Mildred's friends.

Time to shift gears. Raising my hand, I knocked. The conversation inside stopped, as if someone had tossed a blanket on a crackling fire. "Who's there?" Ed asked.

"Hi, Ed. It's Nancy. Can I come in? I have a question." He opened the door and grandly gestured me

123

inside. Harriet was nowhere to be seen, but I could hear the sound of a faucet running in the bathroom.

"How can I help you, my dear?" he asked, his expression showing no signs of stress from his recent battle. Harriet, on the other hand, looked puffy and red as she emerged from the bathroom, patting her face dry with a towel.

"Hello, Nancy," she said, forcing a smile. "I was washing off some sunscreen. It irritates my skin."

"Sorry to bother you both," I said, "but I have a question that might be important to the case. Do either of you know anything about Mildred and Eliza's grandfather? I'm wondering whether Eliza got cut out of an inheritance."

"Yes!" Harriet cried. "Mildred's and Eliza's fathers were twins, but Eliza's father married much later, and that accounts for the age gap between the two cousins."

"So Mildred and Eliza share grandparents on their fathers' side?" I said, just to make sure.

Harriet nodded. "And both Mildred's and Eliza's fathers were cut out of their inheritance because *their* father remarried after his first wife died. He had another family with his second wife. When he finally died, he didn't leave any of his fortune, which was a large one, to his twin sons. He left it to his widow instead, who passed it down to her kids, who were Mildred and Eliza's half cousins."

"Neither Eliza nor Mildred ever saw any of their grandfather's money," Ed added, shaking his head.

Hmm. So Eliza would have no reason to get rid of Mildred, since Mildred didn't have any money either. Casting my mind back to the wording of Eliza's diary, I remembered the line, *If only Mildred and Company weren't in the picture. . . .* The *Company* must refer to her half cousins! But why would Eliza have grouped Mildred with them? I was tempted to confide in Ed and Harriet to get their opinion, but then I would have to tell them I'd sneaked a look at Eliza's diary—and I didn't really want to do that. I mean, maybe they hadn't kidnapped Mildred, and maybe they were on my side, but they were still loose cannons. I especially didn't trust Ed to keep a secret.

As for the *Mildred and Company,* Eliza must have misunderstood the facts. She was only fifteen, after all. Thirty years later, she'd surely understand the truth of what had happened to her grandfather's cash.

I thanked Ed and Harriet and apologized again for bothering them. Then I hurried back to our room, where George and Bess were playing a card game. They looked up expectantly when I entered.

"I'll tell you what happened in a minute," I said, racing to the phone. I punched in Eliza's number at work, and when her voice came on the line, I asked her to tell me the story about the inheritance, so I could confirm that Ed and Harriet had the right story.

"Neither Mildred nor I have a dime," Eliza said sadly after telling me the same story I'd heard just a short time earlier. "Our half cousins have it all. Mildred and I will have to work until we die. Not that I mind, since I like my job. Anyway, what does the inheritance have to do with Mildred's disappearance?"

"I'm not sure," I said.

"Any luck finding Mildred in Maui?" Eliza asked.

"No luck yet, Eliza. I'll let you know the moment anything happens."

"Nice talking to you, Nancy. Bye." I said good-bye and hung up, my heart sinking fast. I couldn't believe it—after all this effort, I was back to square one.

Don't get me wrong; I was thrilled that Eliza wasn't guilty. Crazy as she was, I liked her and wished her well. But there was no getting around the fact that her innocence, plus Jamey's innocence, plus Ed and Harriet's, were a setback to solving this case. I was batting zero here. None of my suspects seemed guilty in the least.

I glanced up at my friends' eager faces. They were dying to know what had happened. Unfortunately the answer was nothing, and I told them so.

"Let's think again about Mildred and her mission,"

I suggested, trying to steer the case back to basics. "She came to Hawaii to research the Night Marchers. She'd been talking to Jamey about them. And then she disappeared."

"And then that note popped up," Bess cut in, "which Eliza led you to."

"That's basically what we know," George said.

"You know," I said, thinking for a moment, "we know a little bit more than that. Remember Robin Ching's professor—what was his name, Alex? The guy who sat in front of Mildred on the plane."

"You mean that guy we met in the restaurant last night?" Bess asked.

"Yup. Now, if Robin is writing her dissertation on Hawaiian mythology and Alex is her professor, that means he must teach it, or at least know about it. So he probably has some background on the Night Marchers. I'm not sure whether that's important to the case, but at this point any lead is worth following."

Bess held up her hand. "Wait, wait, wait. So are you saying there's a connection between him and Mildred, Nancy?"

"Maybe, because of the Night Marchers. I mean, they're a part of Hawaiian mythology, which seems to be Alex's specialty."

I picked up the phone and punched in the number of the Honolulu police. After identifying myself to

Officer Kona, I asked, "Can you please refresh my memory, Officer Kona? Did the police question everyone sitting near Mildred on the plane, including people who sat in front of her?"

"We did, Nancy," she said. "But only to ask them whether they noticed where Mildred went after she disembarked. The answers, of course, were nos."

"There was a man named Alex who sat in front of her," I said, testing to see whether the police actually had questioned him. "Would you happen to know his last name? I know you don't like to give out phone numbers, but if you could bend your policy, I'd really appreciate it. Mildred might really be in danger."

She hesitated. "His name is Alex Kahilua, spelled K-a-h-i-l-u-a. But I'm afraid I can't give you his number. We keep information like that confidential."

Oh, well. No bending the rules for amateur detectives. But I did learn something: Alex had lied about the police. They *had* questioned him.

Interesting.

Alex was probably in the phone book. And if he wasn't, I could always ask Jamey for his number. He or Robin would probably have it. "Well, thanks," I told Officer Kona after copying down Alex's last name. "I'll be in touch if anything develops."

"Thank you, Nancy," she said, and hung up. I

pulled the phone book out of a nook in the night table and opened it to the *Ks*. *K* was a popular letter in Hawaiian, so I had to scroll carefully through a number of names: Kahilo, Fred . . . Kahiloe, Bettina . . . Kahilua, Alexander. There! I was in luck. Not only was there a phone number listed, but also an address.

I made the call. "Hello?" a man's voice said.

"Oh, hi! This is Nancy Drew. We met last night with Robin and Jamey. Do you remember me?"

"Uh, yeah," he said hesitantly.

"I just wondered—do you by any chance teach a class on Hawaiian folklore?"

"Yes, I do."

"Does that class include stuff about the Night Marchers? I mean, do you study them, by any chance?"

"We study them, among other myths," he said guardedly.

"Remember that woman I asked you about named Mildred? She was writing a book about the Night Marchers."

"I thought I told you last night, I don't remember her!" I held the phone away from my ear as he barked his response.

"But the police told me they questioned you about her, so why'd you tell me they hadn't?" I pressed. "They must have told you she was missing

129

too—but you seemed so surprised when I mentioned she'd disappeared."

"What's this phone call about, anyway? What do you want?" he asked, his voice rising.

I could tell he was about to hang up so I shifted back to the Night Marchers. "I'd like to know more about the Night Marchers. Like, do you think that a real gang could be passing themselves off as ghosts?"

"Why do you want to know? What's it to you?" he cried.

"Well, Mildred is missing. We're trying to find her, and I thought that since she came to Hawaii to research the Night Marchers, you might have an idea of where we should look. Because you're an expert on Hawaiian myths."

"Well, that doesn't make me an expert on missing persons! I've got to go, Nancy. I was about to run out the door to hike on Haleakala when you called." He paused for a moment. "I could call you later."

"Sure." I gave him my cell phone number and hung up.

I looked at my friends. They were staring back at me, wide-eyed.

"What a conversation!" George exclaimed. "I could tell by the tone of your voice that Alex wasn't exactly warm and fuzzy."

"He's no Jamey, obviously," Bess added.

"Alex was incredibly antsy the whole time we talked," I said. "Anyone would try to duck questions from a stranger, but he seemed way more defensive than he needed to be. I have a hunch he may be worth checking out. Plus, last night he pretended the police hadn't questioned him."

"Do you know where he lives?" Bess asked.

"His address is in the phone book," I replied. "It's somewhere in Kula, wherever that is. But he told me he was about to hike up Haleakala. That's the volcano in the center of Maui."

"Yes—the one that towers above us everywhere we go," George declared. "Haleakala is supposed to be awesome." She grabbed a pamphlet on Maui from the desk and began to leaf through it. "It's ten thousand feet above sea level—that's higher than some of the Rockies—and its name means 'house of the sun.' Wow, you can actually hike into the crater! The volcano is dormant, of course."

"Dormant?" Bess echoed. "I like the word *dead* much better when referring to volcanos."

"Then you should stay here and hold down the fort while George and I investigate Haleakala." I glanced at George for her approval. Her elated expression said it all.

"There's no fort to hold down here," Bess countered. "I mean, Jamey, Ed, and Harriet are all off the hook." She frowned, then added, "But at least I can call the police if you guys don't come back in a few hours."

"Alex might be another red herring," I said. "Except he did lie to me. Anyway, he can't avoid my questions so easily on a hiking trail."

Minutes later George and I were racing to the summit of Haleakala. My friend was at the wheel, maneuvering the car at top speed along a winding road with stomach-churning switchbacks, driving as fast as you could go and still stay on the mountain. I tried not to look.

My stomach must be made of iron, because even with all the jolts, I was able to read my guidebook as we drove. A photo of one of Haleakala's native endangered plants, silversword, caught my eye because of its cluster of long greenish-gray spikes. The book told me the leaves were firm. It looked more lethal than pretty.

"I wonder what Alex's motive could be?" George said as she screeched around another curve.

"Probably something to do with the Night Marchers, but what?" I forgot to check my watch, but the drive took a while. I could feel the temperature dropping as we climbed higher and higher. Once on the summit, we parked and climbed out of the car.

The view was awesome. Far below us lay the green sugarcane and pineapple fields of Maui. Even farther down, the surf broke on the shore, looking like tiny threads of white lace. And in front of us, jutting from the top of a ring of clouds, was the peak of another volcano shimmering in the chilly blue air.

George and I grabbed our sweatshirts from the backseat of the car. Knowing the altitude of Haleakala in advance, we'd brought them along, but it had been hard to imagine that anything could be this cold on tropical Maui. We shivered in our shorts.

I wished I had more time to admire the view, but I had to find Alex. Shielding my eyes from the sun, I scanned the few tourists wandering around the observation area. He was nowhere to be seen.

"That volcano is active," a young woman with a camera told us, pointing to the volcano facing us. "It's on the Big Island across the water."

"Active?" George repeated curiously. "As in, spewing lava?"

The woman nodded. "I think there's always a low amount of lava coming out of it in certain places."

"How do we hike into the Haleakala crater?" I asked, keeping my mind on Alex.

"There's a trail over there," the woman said, pointing to our left.

"Thanks." As George and I hurried toward it, we

passed a sign describing the geology of Haleakala. George stayed to check it out while I jogged to the rim of the crater, scanning the slope inside for any sign of a hiker. Not a soul was in sight.

A trail snaked down into a weird lunar landscape with only a couple of silverswords to break up the barren scene. I couldn't see the whole crater because mist covered part of it, but the earth inside was black and red, probably from lava. Could Alex be hiking in a pocket of mist? I leaned forward beyond an iron railing to get a better view over the steep slope.

Something thudded against my back—and it felt a lot like a couple of hands. I struggled to regain my balance, my arms pinwheeling—but I'd been leaning too far. I sailed over the edge of the crater, a spiky silversword twenty feet below me!

14

Sneaking In

A **rocky ledge jutted** out beside me. I had no time to think—just grab. Rocks shifted on the ledge, and pebbles and dust fell onto my head as I clutched it. But the ledge was way too loose for me to hold for long. In a moment one of the rocks would slip. Where was George?

I called her name. The rocks made ominous groaning sounds. I was hanging by my fingertips. "George!" I shouted again, trying my best to keep panic from my voice.

The spikes of the silversword gleamed in the sunlight below me. The plant was awesome-looking, like some alien vegetation, but it wasn't called a silversword for nothing. Plunging onto it from twenty feet above would not be my idea of fun.

"George!" I shouted again as dust rained onto my head. And then she was there, leaping down the trail to the ledge and bending toward me. "George, these stones won't hold much longer!"

Just as the rocks I was gripping fell away, George grabbed my wrist. "Don't worry, Nancy," she groaned, "I've got you." She dug her heels into the cliff for support. "You won't fall, but I'm not sure I can pull you all the way up." I hung in midair above the crater, with only George's strong grasp to keep me from crashing onto the rocks and the silversword. If only I had some leverage for my feet!

"Help!" George shouted, aiming her voice at the crater's rim. Turning back to me, she said, "Nancy, when I was running to help you, I saw Alex. He was getting into a rusty white car."

My heart sank. If Alex had taken Mildred to his house, he might be tempted to move her to some other hiding place, knowing that we're closing in. Could we ever catch up to him?

And more importantly, at that moment: How long would I be stuck in midair limbo?

"Help!" George screamed again. Suddenly a park ranger appeared beside her, holding a rope.

"I heard all this yelling," he said. "What's going on? Did someone fall?" He gaped as he saw me dangling in George's grip. Crawling flat onto the ledge, he leaned over and tied the rope securely around my waist. Once the knot was tight, he tugged on the rope, hauling me onto the ledge while George did her best to steady me. With my belly scraping over the stones, I wiggled my way to safety at the base of the ledge.

"Thank you," I said breathlessly once we were back on the rim. I dusted off my hands. I was a little scraped up, but basically all right.

"What happened, young lady?" the ranger asked, peering at me as if I'd done something stupid. "You're supposed to stay inside the railing, unless you're hiking into the crater."

"I was on my way into the crater when I was pushed," I explained. "And the person who pushed me may be dangerous."

The ranger's jaw dropped. I told him quickly about Mildred's disappearance and that Alex may have hidden her somewhere, though I wasn't sure why. "Alex lives in Kula, and I wonder whether Mildred is at his house," I said. "Alex may have suspected that I was on to him, so when he spotted me here, he decided to push me and stop my investigation. I could've hurt myself badly if I'd fallen."

"You're telling me," the ranger said, nodding grimly.

I pulled out my pocket notebook where I'd

scribbled Alex's address and showed it to the ranger. "Would you be able to direct me to this address?"

The ranger gave me directions. Then he frowned, studying our faces with a troubled look. "Girls," he added, "please wait for me to call the police. Give them a chance to get there first. I don't want either of you hurt. Obviously we're dealing with a dangerous criminal." He hurried toward the ranger station to make his call. "Fifteen minutes and then you can go, girls," he barked before going inside. "The Maui police are fast. I'm sure they'll be there by then."

Fifteen minutes? Forget about it! I wasn't going to wait five. Not when Mildred might be in danger. Who knew what Alex would do when the police descended on his house, possibly with sirens blaring? No, it would be wiser to sneak in ahead of the police. Then George and I would have backup against Alex.

George and I didn't waste a moment. While the ranger was still in his station, we jumped into the car and drove off, with George at the wheel. She'd really got the knack of those switchbacks on our way up, and she skillfully maneuvered the sharpest corners on our way down at top speed. Just as the ranger had told us, Kula was partway down Haleakala's slope, and its temperature hovered between the tropical heat of the beach and the chill of Haleakala, reminding me of the brisk San Francisco air.

I checked the address in my notebook. "One eighteen Papaya Tree Drive, George," I said, scanning the ranger's directions. "It's right after Mango Tree Drive. There!"

We turned onto a quiet street lined with trees. Houses were set far apart from one another and hidden from the road behind tall hedges. "There it is, one eighteen," I said as we approached a green mailbox with the driveway opening beyond it on the right. "Wait! Don't go in. Let's park the car along the road."

George pulled the car onto the grassy shoulder of the road, and we climbed out. A narrow gap the perfect size for a roaming dog sliced through the hedge beside us. It was a bit tight for a human, but George and I snuck through it anyway. Once inside, we crept along the hedge, skirting the front yard. The small dark wood house had sliding glass doors and a pineapple field out back. The hedge, trees, and field were all hidden from the neighbors' view.

I tensed. I'd just seen the driveway, and I didn't like its looks. A rusty white car lurked there like a blot on the landscape. I'd been hoping Alex wouldn't be here and Mildred would be. I crossed my fingers that she was inside and okay. "George," I whispered, "let's peek in the front window."

We left the shadow of the hedge behind and crept

into the open yard. So far, so good. Hunkering down, we reached the house with no problem and scrambled into the low shrubbery in front of a picture window. Inside was a living room with dirty beige carpeting and a sofa to match. Books and papers were strewn everywhere.

"Do you think there was a struggle?" George asked nervously.

I shrugged. "Doubt it. I bet he's just a slob."

George cracked a smile, then pointed to our right. "Look, Nancy—stairway to an upstairs deck. We can look through the second-floor windows."

"Excellent!"

George and I tiptoed up the steps to a lanai with a few tumbledown deck chairs haphazardly thrown around it. Immediately facing us was a sliding screen door, and we wasted no time peeking through.

It took us a moment to absorb the sight, but once we did, George and I traded looks. A gray-haired woman lay on a bed with her eyes closed. She stirred slightly as Alex stood over her. He was turned three-quarters away from us, so he couldn't see our silhouettes against the screen, but we could see his brow knitting as he stared at her. Then he bent toward the night table, grabbed a glass of water, and pressed it to her lips.

"Mildred!" he cried. "Mildred!" And he gently slapped her cheeks. I didn't dare whisper to George because my voice would carry through the screen, but I didn't get the feeling that Alex was going to hurt her.

"Look," I mouthed, nudging George. Alex took a cloth from the night table and moistened it in the water. Then he placed it over Mildred's head. Every now and then he squeezed droplets of water into her open lips.

Mildred groaned, and her eyes flew open.

"Now," I whispered to George, sliding open the screen.

Alex whirled around at the noise, but I ignored him. "Mildred," I said, "I'm Nancy Drew, a friend of your cousin, Eliza. My friend George Fayne and I are here to help you. The police are on their way."

"What? Where am I?" she said, frowning. "What do you mean, the police are coming, dear? Is something the matter?"

Then her gaze shifted to Alex—and understanding crossed her face.

"Oh, I feel terrible," Mildred said, rubbing her forehead. "Who are you—and what did you do to me?"

Alex slumped down on a nearby chair and dropped his head into his hands. I relaxed and shot a look at George. She smiled back at me. Alex was clearly no threat, as long as we didn't turn our backs. The word *police* seemed to take the fire out of him.

But to Mildred he had been a threat.

"Alex," I began, "before the police get here, it would be great if you would answer some questions."

"Like why did I kidnap a helpless old lady?" he said bitterly.

"Uh, yeah. Was it something to do with the Night Marchers?" I asked.

"You got it," Alex replied. He stared at me with an expression of surprised respect. "On the plane to Honolulu, I overheard Mildred speaking to Jamey about her writing project. I was worried that her book would compete with mine."

"Are you writing a book too?" I asked.

"Yes, and I'm trying to get university tenure," he explained. "I'm desperate for it, in fact—I'm deeply in debt, and need the steady income. My book is also a mystery about the Night Marchers, and if there was another book on the same subject as mine, I'd be ruined. So I lured Mildred to my house by promising to show her actual pictures of the Night Marchers. But those photos never existed."

"Shame on you, young man!" Mildred cried, sitting up in bed. "How did you ever think you'd stop my book? By giving me amnesia?"

"I never meant to hurt you," Alex said in a pleading tone. "Once you were safely here, I knew I could distract you. You'd put down your laptop, and while you were looking at pictures of Hawaii, I'd sneak your computer, boot it up, and delete all the files on your book. Then I'd return it before you realized it had even been missing."

"You're nothing but a cheat and a scoundrel!" Mildred said, her dimpled cheeks flushing pink. "I don't care how desperate for money you are—what you did is downright evil. There is no excuse." I was happy to see some color returning to her face. "Besides, do you take me for a fool who doesn't back up her work?"

"Your backup disk was in your computer drive," Alex said, casually removing a disk from his pocket and handing it back to Mildred. Mildred took it from him and stared at it lovingly as if it was a long-lost child, which I guess to her it was.

He shrugged. "I was willing to take the chance that you had another backup disk at home. You see, I wasn't expecting to wipe out all traces of your book. But without your files to work with on this trip, your book would get delayed and wouldn't compete with mine. You could always suspect me later, but you'd have no proof."

"All right—that's all fine, but I'd like to know

what you've done to Mildred," George said. "You say you were planning to sneak her computer away so you could delete files, but you've kept her here all this time, and she's obviously not in good health."

Mildred had lain back down, and George was right—she didn't look too well.

Alex's face grew as sickly pale as the carpet. "My plan failed. Like I told you I, I'd never planned to hurt Mildred, just to sneak her computer away for a moment so I could delete the files. But she watched it like a hawk, so I had to knock her out. I meant for her to be unconscious for only a few minutes, but . . ." His voice trailed off.

"What did you hit her with?" I asked.

"My portable phone," Alex replied miserably. "The blow wasn't very hard, but it hurt Mildred more than I realized it would. I've been trying to nurse her back to health ever since. This morning she started to stir and even swallow. She took some water, soda, and a little bit of chicken soup. She opened her eyes for a while before I left for Haleakala, but it wasn't till now that she really perked up."

This was really perked up? Mildred must have been in terrible shape before now.

"I'm not such a bad guy, really," Alex added.

"Humph!" Mildred said, raising a frail hand to her forehead. "What do you mean, you're not so bad? I feel like I've been hit with a brick!"

"Alex," I said, "did you lure me to Haleakala on purpose? Just so you could injure me and get me off your track?"

Alex's stony expression told me what no words of his ever would admit.

"You're really *not* a nice guy, Alex, no matter what you claim," I finished.

I turned to Mildred and explained that Ed and Harriet had sent us to find her. "What dear friends I have!" she said, clasping her hands together thankfully. "I suppose they were also quite worried about the book I'm writing for them—I think they're expecting it to do very well." She smirked. "What wonderful girls you are for figuring out where I was, though. Who knows what would have happened if I'd been left alone with *that* snake?" Narrowing her eyes at Alex, she added, "I bet you were hoping my concussion would blot out my memory of your attack—and of my book, too! You were hoping you'd deleted the files in my *brain*."

One look at Alex's guilty expression told me that Mildred was right. "As it happens," Mildred continued defiantly, "this whole experience has given me even *more* ideas. Just wait till my next mystery novel comes out!"

George and I laughed, while Alex remained silent.

"But what about the note? Did you write it, Alex?" I asked.

Alex nodded. "I forged Mildred's writing and planted the note during a quick trip to Oahu when I went to speak at a conference. I'd overheard Mildred talking about Eliza on the plane, so I called to Eliza from outside her house, pretending to be a ghost. I gave her directions to the note, hoping to turn suspicion away from myself."

"But Eliza didn't find it—I did," I said. "I think she felt so freaked out when she looked for it alone that she couldn't concentrate." I cast my mind back to the night we found the note. The ringing noise I'd thought was a dream must have really been Alex's fake ghostly voice. Eliza must have confused his directions, which is why she searched the prickly jungle trail as well as the historic site.

"Poor Eliza!" Mildred declared, glaring at Alex. "You really *are* a miserable worm of a person!"

Sirens sounded in the driveway. Within a few minutes the police were leading a handcuffed Alex away, while emergency technicians bundled Mildred into an ambulance to take her to the hospital for observation. "Don't you worry, girls," Mildred said brightly before the technicians shut the ambulance door. "I feel fine. I can't wait to write my next mystery. You'll figure into it big, I promise!"

· · · ·

Back at the Blue Wave Hotel, George, Bess, Harriet, Ed, and I sat on a terrace overlooking the beach, drinking pineapple-coconut juice and snacking on freshly made taro chips. The glassy sea reflected the pink sunset. The surf was as calm as I was, now that I knew Mildred was finally safe.

"We have a confession to make, girls," Ed said, his eyes twinkling.

"What's that?" Bess said skeptically, shooting a worried look his way.

"Harriet, Mildred, and I are all part of a mystery writers' group in San Francisco. When Harriet and I first met you, Nancy, we followed you around in hopes of getting a book idea. We knew you'd find a mystery sooner or later, and once you did, Mildred would write it, and Harriet and I would have published it. Featuring you as the detective, of course."

"But when we discovered that Mildred was actually missing," Harriet cut in, "we realized we had our own mystery on our hands, and we needed you, Nancy, to solve it. Which of course you did. So three cheers for Nancy Drew and her fabulous detective work!" She raised her glass in a toast.

Bess's face flushed with relief as we all clinked glasses. She seemed to breathe a little easier with this explanation of why Ed and Harriet had been

147

following us, and I did too. Another case solved.

Leaning back in my chair, I marveled at the scenery around us. Hawaii was truly beautiful, and I was excited about having a little time to enjoy it before heading home. Well—unless I stepped into another mystery. And as long as Harriet, Ed, and Mildred were around, it seemed distinctly possible!

REDISCOVER THE CLASSIC MYSTERIES OF NANCY DREW

Think it would be fun to get stuck on a deserted island with the guy you sort of like? Well, try adding the girl who gets on your nerves big-time (*and* who's crushing on the same guy), the bossiest kid in school, your annoying little brother, and a bunch of other people, all of whom have their own ideas about how things should be done. Oh, and have I mentioned that there's no way off this island, and no one knows where you are?

Still sound great? Didn't think so.

Now all I have to worry about is getting elected island leader, finding something to wear for a dance (if you can believe that), and surviving a hurricane, all while keeping my crush away from Little Miss Priss. Oh, and one other teeny-tiny little thing: surviving.

Get me outta here!

Read all the books in the Castaways trilogy:

#1 Worst Class Trip Ever

#2 Weather's Here, Wish You Were Great

#3 Isle Be Seeing You